FEVER MAIDEN

Elane Peridot

FEVER MAIDEN

First paperback edition 2022
Published by Flower Garden Press

ISBN-13: 978-1-958550-01-4

Printed in the United States of America
Cover Art by DLR Cover Designs

FLOWER GARDEN
PRESS

To my husband and our beautiful daughters.
Y'all are my greatest treasure.

CONTENTS

People almost always keep secrets for selfish reasons. Papa had a secret...but Papa kept his secret out of love.

This is a story about love.

CHAPTER ONE

Coal Miner's Daughter

One thing was for certain, the girl named Scarlett-Rain Manchester was a recluse, and she was very much content. The unforgiving Tennessee wilderness was a cloak, and she wrapped herself within the stretching timber forests and cold rivers like a tiny nature sprite. The gold and copper landscape draped around her pale frame as if it were a gown made for a special queen. Only, she wasn't a royal at all, and sometimes, the trees laughed at her childish dreams as their skinny branches tore at her bushy, black hair—"*dark as coal,*" Papa always said, and he was an expert on the matter.

Papa's skin was light brown, but for the first few years of her life, Scarlett-Rain believed he was a black man. It was said the coal mines had a way of changing men's appearances, and this much had always been true about Papa. Day after day, he would hike back home from the mines with a familiar, dirty blackness soaking his skin and clothes. Jokingly, he would attempt to kiss Mama by the wood-burning stove, but she wouldn't have it. With a squeal, she'd swat him away with her old spoon, and his deep chuckles would echo through the quiet, little cabin. This was peaceful music to the sensitive ears of Scarlett-Rain.

Life in the Tennessee wilds was perilous, at times, but this fact was hidden away from the Manchesters' only child. Scarlett-Rain was protected with an impenetrable shield of love, and she was ignorant of the dangers hiding in the lands around her home. For fifteen years, she had walked through the cool shade of the woods with as much quiet pride as a southern princess. As far as she was concerned, Papa and Mama ruled these lands, for who was there to say otherwise?

Papa owned lots of land, though he was poor. It was prideful to discuss one's own possessions, no matter how small or great, and Mr. Dillon Manchester was never one to brag. There were rumors that Papa had won the land in a lucky card game many years back, but Scarlett-Rain didn't believe such nonsense. Papa had never been a gambling man, not since she'd known him, at least.

In Tennessee, there was a well-known understanding. Land was more valuable than money—more valuable than anything, according to most folks—and Scarlett-Rain saw how much her papa loved it. Sometimes, she bickered with the wilderness, as if it were a sibling alive with normal jealousies. "You silly ol' tree!" she argued one day. "Papa don't love you more than me!" With a loud cackle, the wind responded by knocking a small, gray branch on top of her head.

For the most part, the Manchesters were very much alone in their part of the wilderness, and they liked it this way. It was a thirty-minute walk to their closest neighbors' house, and the Springfield family was an odd bunch, to say the least. Like most folks, they kept to themselves, and Scarlett-Rain only saw them in the warmer months when Papa took his family to the little church in the hills. The Springfields were graced with three sons, larger than oxen, and a shriveled, little daughter named Echo. She was thirteen years old, two years younger than Scarlett-Rain, but she looked no older than ten. Whether or not they were friends, Scarlett-Rain didn't know, but Echo was more than willing to stick her tongue out at her neighbor during church, which seemed friendly enough.

"A *waste!*" Echo's blonde mother, Patty Springfield, would hiss to the other church ladies regarding her own daughter. "Havin' a girl is such a *waste* in this territory, and to think how hard I prayed for a fourth son! God doesn't hear my prayers!"

Scarlett-Rain figured out long ago that Patty Springfield and her husband, Willy, were people to be feared. Sometimes, Papa's land whispered frightening stories to Scarlett-Rain about their closest neighbors. "*A witch!*" the cold river laughed one day. "*Mrs. Patty Springfield is a witch, and that dumb-lookin' ol' Mr. Willy is a warlock from the Devil.*"

It was easy to imagine Echo's daddy as a wizard, because he was always drinking strange potions. Papa even said, somewhere on Mr. Springfield's property, there was a hideout where the wizard mixed his own potions. Scarlett-Rain shuddered. She didn't like that story.

"Shut up!" she hissed to the river like a fed-up big sister. "Stop tryin' ter scare me!"

The restless, young river appeared to shrug with lively waves, and it fell silent for a few days.

The solitude of the Tennessee wilderness was comforting and familiar, and though Scarlett-Rain sometimes wished for a brother or sister to keep her company, her mangy dog and the chattering woods had always been enough to fill that charcoal-colored void. Believe it or not, the forest was a talkative, and often grumpy, entity to those who were lonely enough to listen, and Scarlett-Rain could hear its amusing banter with the sharpest ears in the territory.

Caliber, the Manchesters' dog, was an old, cowardly thing—more fur than muscle. He was never quite the same after Papa accidentally shot him years back, yet he managed to retain his wolf-like pride. Daily, he walked lazily across the Manchesters' land with the same, never-ending delusion that it was he, the mighty dog, who owned everything. Some days, Scarlett-Rain would argue with the fuzzy half-breed who insisted on trailing after her everywhere she went. "Caliber, yer worse than a grouchy, old grandpappy!" she'd declare, and the wolf-dog would just grunt.

One crisp evening in early September, Scarlett-Rain and Caliber were hiking through the bronze, rusty forest, and the tall, majestic timbers began to groan with loud agony. With wide, hazel eyes—browner than golden tree bark mixed with mossy-green river droplets—the

Manchester girl stopped in her tracks to take in her surroundings.

Her soggy boots were stuck an inch deep in mud as she listened to a quiet moan of panic emerge from the river's autumn song. Little, trickling streams rushed with an unrecognizable cold fury, and Caliber barked as a skittish squirrel leaped from a branch and missed. The pale-yellow grass quivered beside heavy tree roots, and the hills woke with an angry grumble.

"Somethin's wrong," Scarlett-Rain said to her gray, bear-like dog, and the cool wind kissed her smooth, porcelain cheeks in agreement.

With a chipper howl, Caliber bounded across the rocky forest after his master. Razor-sharp leaves and branches, like whips, cut Scarlett-Rain's skin as she hurried to the lookout. It was her secret place, for what nature princess didn't have a royal thinking spot of her very own? Ha! She could hardly call herself a girl without a place to build enormous dreams and blow away wishes with soft, brown rose petals.

It wasn't far to the lookout, and when she spotted that large, cold and wrinkled rock jutting out the edge of the hillside (like an ugly piece of shrapnel), her chilly breath stopped. The trees were suddenly silent, and the rivers pretended to be asleep. Little rabbits and squirrels hid away in their dens, fearful of the giant rock overlooking the crimson and topaz landscape below.

With a twisted face toward the trees, Scarlett-Rain boldly marched toward her rock as her old boots stomped atop crackling leaves. Caliber nipped at her dark, moldy-green dress and cream apron. Softly, she patted his head and bravely held her foot over the rock, as if daring Papa's land to protest. To her rebellious delight, the wilderness gasped with a sudden, fierce wind, just as she predicted it would.

"Shut up, you miserable coward!" she hissed to the protective forest, and Caliber tried to yank her back by biting her woolen gown. Gently, she kicked her pet away. "Yer just as bad as the blasted woodland!" she told him while waving her hand toward the treetops. "Neither of y'all is my friend anymore!"

Of course, she regretted it immediately after she said it, and the fragile rivers burst into steady tears more pathetic than a teenage girl.

"Hmph!" said Scarlett-Rain as she turned away from her only two friends in the world. They would get over it soon enough, for who else did they have to talk to? Who else was sensitive enough to hear their mysterious voices?

With a graceful thrust, she threw her skinny body against the very end of the goliath rock. She was just close enough to the edge to make Caliber yelp with fright, and she grinned crookedly at his plea. With a mother's embrace, the cool, delicate breeze tried to lure the girl back as it ran its smooth, ghostly fingers through her long, thick hair, but she swiped it away.

With eyes like the timberlands, Scarlett-Rain peered over the ledge, and gravity swept itself away all at once. Smiling with her chapped lips slightly open, she soaked in the magenta September air as the miles of bare fields and copper meadows far below grinned up at her. In the distance, shadowy hills, like baby mountains, rose to meet the bold evening sky, and the hand of God stretched down to hold them with rolling, silver clouds. A little purple martin sat chirping on an overhanging limb, just above the girl's head, and she looked up at him. He seemed to be admiring The Creator's handiwork with fussy excitement, and Scarlett-Rain giggled as he sped away through the air.

With a heavy sigh, the dark orange sun cast its rays against the pastures below, as if trying to reveal a secret to the Manchester girl. With a startled gasp, Scarlett-Rain saw the great disturbance—the fear that shook the hills and the wilds, the noisy ruckus that scared her proud wolf-dog. Riding along dozens of scribbled ruts etched within the meadows were hundreds of rickety carriages. The long lines of tired horses pulling little buggies and covered wagons seemed endless to the child-like eyes of Scarlett-Rain. For a long moment, she was unable to breathe, and the land shuddered.

"Settlers!"

Quickly, she pulled away from the dangerous ledge while gathering her long skirts.

"Come on, Caliber!" she said while thumping him on the head. "We gotta go tell Papa and Mama!"

The dog jumped at her command, much too pleased to have his master back from the hazardous lookout point. The rivers, still hurt from Scarlett-Rain's ex-friendship, gave her the silent treatment. She huffed while rolling her round feminine eyes, which were hidden beneath thick lashes. Rivers were temperamental beings, rarely forgetting a wrong, and memories just soaked into their muddy banks, forever to be remembered.

"Stop bein' so sensitive!" Scarlett-Rain called out to the land as she ran, and for reasons unknown to her, a sudden rush of forbidden excitement shot through her pale blue veins like a bolt of lightning from an unknown thundercloud. What adventures would these foreigners bring, and what treacherous stories were concealed within their covered wagons? The rusty leaves cracked and popped beneath the girl's unladylike boots, and the stubborn trees shouted after her.

"*Don't get involved!*" The song was all around her, whispering through her ears with the same cool force of a cautious grandmother. "*It's wise to be alone.*"

"Shut up!" Scarlett-Rain yelled back, and the tall pines and oaks went as silent as the wounded rivers.

CHAPTER TWO

Little Girls Must Grow Up

In familiar silence, Scarlett-Rain helped her mama, Pleasant Manchester, rekindle the fire in the small, family cabin. The warm, spicy smell of cinnamon clouded the comfortable heat emanating from the blazing logs, and Scarlett Rain's slender mother smiled at her daughter with naturally blushed cheeks. Mama's eyes were greener than Tennessee treetops in May, and her long braided hair was both yellow and brown, like a perfect mixture of wheat and gingerbread. She was small and dainty, yet stronger than she appeared, and she could chop firewood with just as much ease as Papa. Like her daughter, Pleasant Manchester was quiet and content. The land bowed to her the same way it bowed to Scarlett-Rain, and she spoke to animals and rivers with graceful blue songs only the very wise could understand.

With a slight sigh, she placed her pale, freckled arm on her hip and glanced out the window to search for Papa. Her long, cotton dress was silvery white, and the apron around her middle was only slightly darker—more of a mustard seed tone.

"It's so good ta have cinnamon biscuits again," she said happily as she made her way over to the wood-burning stove. "Papa has certainly spoiled us this year."

With a pinkish-gray smile, she handed her daughter a biscuit, and Scarlett-Rain sat down, in the center of the room, at the family table to eat. Caliber moaned from somewhere inside a shadowy corner of the house, and Pleasant called him over.

Faking something reminiscent of cuteness, the dog wolfed down a biscuit of his own, then licked Pleasant's soft, bare face. He looked up at Scarlett-Rain, who was shaking her head, and made his way back to his smelly corner.

"What a big baby," the girl mumbled as she chewed her buttery, sweet snack, and Mama laughed.

"Honey," said Pleasant as she began to set out flowery blue and white plates (her favorite dishes). "How would ya like ta wear yer pretty lavender dress tomorrow when we go inta town together? It's been a while since you've worn it."

Scarlett-Rain nodded. "Okay."

Mama finished setting out the dishes, then disappeared into the bedroom she shared with Papa. After a few moments, she returned to the dining table while holding up a pale purple dress with roses printed across the fabric. Her long fingers softly caressed the cotton. "This was the dress you was baptized in," she said, reminiscing. "That was a happy day, but you were so cold! Remember?"

"Yes'm," replied Scarlett-Rain. "Papa was cold, too, when he dunked me in the creek, but he didn't complain. It was only October, but it snowed the very next day."

"You were eleven then," Mama said, still remembering. "My, how time goes so fast." She looked at her daughter and smiled. "Well, come on now, Honey. Put it on!"

More than happy to play dress-up with Mama, Scarlett-Rain set down her biscuit and shimmied out of her clothes. Mama was humming as she helped her daughter into the dress. Suddenly, she went quiet.

Scarlett-Rain glanced down at two tall, skinny legs sticking out the bottom of the gown. Mama didn't attempt to button the back...

"Oh..."

For a long moment, Pleasant examined her daughter with a strange sadness clouding her fern-green gaze, and her soft, melodious voice chimed timidly with both joy and fear. "You've grown so fast... You're almost a woman now. This dress won't fit a woman, Scarlett-Rain..."

Scarlett-Rain's hazel stare, like pine trees and muddy rivers, widened, and her mother just sighed. The fire hummed close by, and crickets outside the windows began to sing to the peach and sandstone-colored dusk. With little teardrops dripping down her cheeks, Pleasant grasped her daughter's cool hand.

"You sprung up," she said with almost a shattered tune (for Mama's voice always sounded like music). "You ain't my little baby anymore."

Scarlett-Rain wasn't sure why, but Mama's words were more painful than a whipping. *Did it hurt to grow up?* It must because Scarlett-Rain felt the sharp sting of adulthood in a frightening instant. Her throat tightened, and stupid nervousness engulfed her tiny body.

"I'm...sorry, Mama," she said, almost pleadingly.

Pleasant shook her head, tears streaming down her pale, brown-speckled face. Her hands were rough and cold, and they held onto her daughter's fingers as if the firmness of her grip would keep childhood preserved.

"Don't be sorry, baby girl!" she said, and Scarlett-Rain had to look away from her mama's broken face. "It brings me so much joy ta see the woman you've become...but it's sad, too. Life's like that. Joy and sadness go hand in hand." She smiled. "Before I know it, you'll be gettin' married!"

Caliber moaned from his dark corner.

The word *"married"* jolted inside Scarlett-Rain's tummy, and she thought she might be sick. Desperately, without meeting Mama's minty, clover eyes, she fumbled over something to say—*anything* to escape the heartache that impending womanhood was causing Mama.

"Nonsense, Mama. You know I don't talk ter...*boys*."

A long breath escaped Pleasant's tight, wet lips as she patted her daughter's hand.

"You don't know it, Darlin', but yer very beautiful. Pretty soon, a nice young man's gonna notice, and you'll be head over heels...in *love*."

More tears fell from Mama's eyes, and Scarlett-Rain couldn't understand her mother's sadness and joy complimenting each other in perfect musical unison.

With something like a doggish chuckle, Caliber grunted when Mama mentioned *"love,"* and Scarlett-Rain felt her little-girl spirit freeze over like a winter river.

"Love?" The word was harsh and grating against her tongue and cheeks. It felt illogically threatening, like an attack on her childhood. She was happy the land couldn't hear Mama's gentle conversation. *Oh, how rattled the touchy wilderness would be at the notion of Scarlett-Rain growing up!* She'd never hear the end of it.

With a gasp, she let go of Mama's hand. Feeling faint, she grabbed hold of the sturdy dining table and let out a dry sob.

"Oh, Mama...why does this *growin' up* business gotta be so...hard?" She was trembling, and Mama pitied her with a sweet face full of nature's empathy.

"It's hard for everybody," she said simply, "but it's the Lord's will that we grow and become wiser. I'll teach ya how ta be a woman, Scarlett-Rain. One day, you'll do the same for yer own daughter."

With a cry of love, Mama threw her arms around her only child. *Was Mama sad? Was Mama happy?* Scarlett-Rain didn't know, but she felt an uncomfortable, aching throb chewing at her from within. With an awkward glance, she saw Caliber's glowing eyes staring at her from within the shadows, and there was no sympathy from him, only truth.

There was no knowing how long Pleasant held her there, but before long, Papa's deep voice echoed across the hills, through the woods and into the little, windy holes of the cabin's walls. Mama let go of Scarlett-Rain and giggled with tear-stained, speckled cheeks.

"Papa's home!" they exclaimed, running for the door. Caliber barked and followed them as Pleasant threw open the door.

To Scarlett-Rain's relief, Mama was smiling again with nothing but profound glee on her freckled, dandelion face. Papa's large, dark frame was striding over the pasture, and they could see his familiar pickaxe riding atop his shoulder. His giant heart was light, and a humble song sprang from his blackened lips.

"Fair as a lily, joyous and free.
Light of that little home was she.
Ev'ryone who knew her felt the gentle pow'r,
of Scarlett-Rain, my sweet wildflow'r..."

Pleasant smiled down at Scarlett-Rain. Papa was always inserting their names into songs and changing the lyrics on a whim. He was in a good mood, which meant the mines were friendly to him today. This pleased Scarlett-Rain, for she still had alarming news to give her parents. *Would Mama and Papa welcome the thought of new settlers in the territory, or would they be suspicious, just like the trees, hills and rivers?*

"Howdy there, handsome man!" Mama called out to Papa.

It wasn't long before Dillon Manchester made it to the cabin and swooped his wife into a long, funny kiss. She playfully swatted the back of his dark head, and when he let her go, she had black coal all over her face and lips.

Scarlett-Rain giggled. *Would she ever love someone the way Mama loved Papa?*

CHAPTER THREE

Gold Fever

According to most folks, the Manchesters were timid people. No matter how hard she tried, Scarlett-Rain could not understand this judgment, for their little cabin was always filled with music. Papa could play the banjo better than anyone in the territory, and when he played, his daughter and wife looked upon him as if he were a hero of old. The banjo made a beautiful whiny sound, like a loved baby that never grew old. To Scarlett-Rain, the notes were always brown, like timber or firewood, sturdy log cabins or Papa's skin. The banjo's music was happy and light, and sometimes it was soft and sad. No matter what mood the songs were in, they always told a story, and Scarlett-Rain could feel friendly ghosts reaching out to touch her face.

The night Scarlett-Rain told Papa about the strange settlers entering the land, he had played dancing music after supper. Clapping and spinning arm in arm, Pleasant and her daughter laughed and twirled until their callused feet gave out. The songs were warm and thrilling, and the little cabin was bursting with the same exciting personality of a spring fair. Papa's voice was deep and heavy, and the rhythm carried the same powerful melody of sturdy pickaxes being thrown against stubborn rocks.

When he was finished playing, Dillon hooted and howled with his large, chiseled head thrown back. His sloppy, dark hair was greasy and sweat-filled, and most of his skin and clothes were still covered in the mines' black spit—except for his hands, of course. Mama always made sure his rough, hairy hands were clean as a whistle before they touched her cooking.

"That was wonderful, Papa!" Scarlett-Rain exclaimed, and Mama was still laughing with the same whistling tranquility as a purple martin.

"Well, thank ya, lil' darlin'." Papa was panting and grinning like a grizzly bear. His eyes were dark, like the vast night sky or hot, bitter coffee in a tin cup. Caliber, as usual, was off in the corner by himself, pretending to be a lazy loner, but Scarlett-Rain had easily spotted how his fuzzy, silver ears twitched in time with the music.

With a nervous sigh, Scarlett-Rain pulled a wooden chair from alongside the family dining table and positioned it to face her parents. Slowly, she sat down and watched as Mama tenderly wiped the black smudge from Papa's face with her apron. They were giggling and smiling at each other, and it was easy to view them as children. Love fueled their thoughts and actions. It was so powerful that sometimes Scarlett-Rain could not breathe around them. Their love was a dominant presence, old as a mountain, yet alive as a cool brook. Scarlett-Rain knew the song. It was blue and open, as tasty as a summer sky, and the tune was reminiscent of clear raindrops dripping against spotless glass. She loved their song—that blessed gift from God. It was one of her favorites.

"Papa..." she said, and her voice broke. Dillon's large, square face stared at his daughter, and Pleasant's freckled cheeks turned to meet her, too. They knew something was wrong, and Papa's enormous, muscular arms propped his banjo on the floor beside him.

"Yes, Dear?" Pleasant said, worried, and she walked over to stroke her daughter's long, black hair. Caliber made a foreign noise from his stinky corner as Scarlett-Rain tried to explain.

"I was at the...lookout today, and—"

"Scarlett-Rain!" Mama's hummingbird voice was suddenly shrill and stern. "How many times have we told ya not ta dangle over the edge of that darn cliff?"

"I wasn't danglin', Mama!" She looked at Dillon who was silent as a boulder. He handled anger differently than his wife. When Pleasant was mad, her emotions morphed into pitiful worry, but Papa's irritation always had to simmer for a while, like camp stew in an iron pot.

"Scarlett-Rain—" he began in a tired, disappointed voice.

"I saw settlers!" the girl explained. "Hundreds of 'em! Down in the valley!"

Mama and Papa looked at each other, and Scarlett-Rain couldn't determine what soundless words they exchanged. Caliber let out a non-threatening growl as he sensed their invisible concerns. After what seemed like ages, Papa bowed his head and simply said, "gold."

Mama gasped slightly as her slender fingers lightly touched her pinkish lips.

"What's gold?" Scarlett-Rain blurted, and the fireplace hissed and laughed.

Papa's big face was buried in his even larger hands, and he peeked at his daughter between his dirty fingers. "Gold...is a very rare metal, Honey."

Scarlett-Rain stared at her parents. "I don't understand," she said. "What does it look like?"

Mama laughed. "Well, we ain't never seen it, Baby, but I suppose it looks like..." She looked at Papa as her precious thoughts tried and failed to describe a substance even she didn't fully understand.

"It looks like the sun!" she said at last, and Papa chuckled.

"It's worth more than the sun if that's what ya mean," he stated. "Gold's a hard thing ta describe, but it likes ta live inside of rock. The color is yeller and glitterin', and you'd know it if you saw it." He looked at Scarlett-Rain. "Don'tcha go messin' around with them settlers, pretty gal. Every last one of 'em has the fever."

"Fever?" said Scarlett-Rain. "What fever—"

"Gold fever," Mama answered.

Laughing again, Dillon picked up his instrument and walked over to his daughter. Rubbing the top of her soft black hair, he said, "don't you go worryin' over things like gold. People will tell ya it's the most valuable thing in the world, but it ain't." For a moment, his deep brown eyes rested on his pale wife, then on his little girl, and lastly, on his banjo. Scarlett-Rain wasn't sure why, but she thought she glimpsed sadness in his gaze—or was it love? Sometimes, she mixed up the two.

"Papa, will I ever get ter see gold?" The question slipped out of her lips before she could stop it. All at once, without warning, some brand-new curiosity seized her, and her mind became consumed with images of gleaming yellow rock that looked like the sun.

Dillon's giant body froze. "What kind of a silly question is that?"

Immediately, Pleasant came over to her daughter and knelt before her. Her ivy-green eyes were glistening with immortal youth, and she stroked Scarlett-Rain's soft cheek.

"Yer papa's right," she said. "Keep yer mind on the Lord, and you'll have everythin' ya need."

With a smile, she stood and held out her hand to Scarlett-Rain.

"Come, Honey. Let's go pick ya out a dress ta wear ta town tomorrow. I've been savin' a few of mine just for you."

Scarlett-Rain glanced back at Dillon who was now standing by the window staring out into the darkness.

What was he thinking? she wondered, but it didn't really matter. A new dream stormed inside her thoughts, and she couldn't make it go away. Visions of gold whispered from all around, though she couldn't even comprehend what it was or how it truly looked. It spoke to her with strange promises, and the color yellow took on a whole new meaning. Gold was everywhere Scarlett-Rain looked. It was dancing in the fire. It was twinkling, like tiny balls of light, in the sky. Gold was littered across the autumn leaves and blades of grass below the night's canopy, and if she looked close enough in the mirror, she could see it reflecting back at her from within her own hazel eyes. Caliber growled, for he knew his master's thoughts. She longed to see it, just once. She wished to witness the power that drove the wild settlers into strange, unforgiving territory.

CHAPTER FOUR

Papa's Rival

Morning arrived with a cool whisper of wind through the cabin cracks. Scarlett-Rain's room was a small loft overlooking the main floor of the cabin. Just outside, she could hear the whiny of high-spirited horses. Papa had hitched them to the wagon before he left for work, like he always did when his wife and daughter were going into the nearby town of *Calliway*. Mama was standing on the wooden ladder connected to the loft as she watched her daughter's reflection in the tall vanity mirror. "You look beautiful!" she exclaimed, but Scarlett-Rain just huffed. *Lace. Why did the dress Mama picked for her last night have to be adorned with scratchy lace around the neckline?*

Her pale cheeks flushed as she stared at her skinny, child-like body in the mirror. The long, yellow dress was simple and elegant, but against her wild, black hair, she thought it made her resemble a starving bumblebee. This was a gown made for pretty women, not for ugly girls stuck between the limbo of childhood and adulthood. Feeling embarrassed, Scarlett-Rain fought to hold back a tear.

With a sweet smile, Mama stepped off the ladder and walked over to her daughter. Saying nothing, she began to brush out the tangles from the girl's long, thick hair. Scarlett-Rain looked at Pleasant over her puffy sleeve. "Mama, this dress looks purtier on you."

"Nonsense." She glanced at the girl's pastel reflection. "This is the gown I wore when I first met yer pa. It's yers now, Baby." She smiled again, pink and memory-filled.

With a solemn expression, Scarlett-Rain studied the girlish reflection of the skinny bumblebee staring back at her. She could never be as lovely as Mama. That much was clear, but for a hopeful second, she dared to wonder if a boy could ever find her attractive.

"There! All done!" Mama sang as she set the brush on Scarlett-Rain's quilted bed. "I declare, Darlin', ya truly are the most gorgeous gal in all of Tennessee!"

Scarlett-Rain shuffled her old boots beneath her dress. Obviously, Mama was blind.

With a sigh, she grabbed her white crochet shawl off the bed and followed Pleasant down the ladder. As they left the cabin, Caliber ran after them and jumped into the wagon with king-like pride. Of course, he noticed his master's new attire, and he quickly approved of it with a gentle sniff.

With feminine grace, Pleasant took the reins. Her daughter frowned in the seat beside her, and swiftly, they were off. The early morning fog evaporated as they rode along the sloppy wagon-rut roads. The September air was crisp with the promise of an early winter, and the trees panicked when they saw Scarlett-Rain adorned in princess clothes.

"*She's leavin' us!*" The timbers shouted with cracking voices.

Scarlett-Rain rolled her eyes.

"*She's never comin' back!*" The rivers sang together in perfect harmony.

"*They're tryin' to turn her into a woman!*" The winds howled. "*She'll never hear our voices again!*"

Within the veil of her bushy hair, Scarlett-Rain clasped her hands over her ears.

"Fallin' in love with a boy will end your childhood—"

"You'll never play again—"

"You'll have to leave yer Mama and Papa—"

Suddenly, the hills spoke with a deep, sleepy yawn. *"It's all for the best. Scarlett-Rain must grow up. She must live the life she was born to live."*

The bickering that erupted from the wilderness was too much. Scarlett-Rain could almost feel the wet breeze clawing at her mama's pastel yellow dress, trying to hold her back. Rusty leaves swirled across dew-sprinkled blades of grass, and the birds' autumn music sounded angrier than usual.

"You'll forget about us!" sang a squirrel as it threw an acorn against a rock.

The hills chuckled. *"They always forget sooner or later. It's the way of things. It's His plan."*

For an entire hour, Scarlett-Rain listened to the mindless squabbling of the forest. To her surprise, Caliber didn't have much to say on the matter. For most of the trip, he stuck his giant head between the Manchester ladies and breathed happily in Scarlett-Rain's face. When the hills spoke, he agreed with a lazy dog groan, then stuck his sour tongue right next to

Scarlett-Rain's nose. Sometimes, Mama sang, and her angelic, crystal voice filled her daughter's heart with warmth. She loved Mama's music. It was a guiding lullaby, forever pointing in the right direction, and the morning sun filled her face with eternal youth.

If Scarlett-Rain had known she was actually going to fall head-over-heels *in love* that day, she never would have hopped into that wagon. She would have stayed behind and let Papa's land coddle her for the rest of her days. However, the hills had been correct in their drowsy wisdom. Scarlett-Rain had to grow up. It was life's way. So, with comfortable bliss, the Manchesters' wagon pulled up next to the Calliway Mercantile, and Scarlett-Rain was oblivious to the plan God, Himself, had purposed for her.

Mama stepped down from her seat, and Caliber hopped out after her. Pleasant's chestnut bonnet couldn't hide the long strands of wheat-colored hair draping down her shoulders. She reached up for her daughter, but Scarlett-Rain shook her head. Shyness was a horrible disease, and it reared its head at the worst of moments. Despite Mama's pleading eyes, Scarlett-Rain just couldn't budge. *What if someone laughed at her in the mercantile? What if some rude settler called her a bumblebee?* She shuddered. Of course, everyone would notice her awkward ascent into womanhood. The fine dress wouldn't fool anyone. Underneath Mama's beautiful gown, she was still a scrawny, quiet child. *Oh, how humiliating it would be for someone to point out her failures!*

Biting her lip, she clutched the wagon seat and shook her head at Mama's outstretched hand. With a sigh, Pleasant lowered it. "Darlin', please come inta the mercantile with me ta buy our supplies."

Scarlett-Rain shook her head, fighting back senseless tears. Somewhere close by, brown guitar music hummed through the air. Folks were walking all around the wide dirt road stretching down the town's center, but no one noticed the comfortable song. It sailed right across the town of Calliway without a care in the world, but Scarlett-Rain heard it. Her head whipped around in the direction of the melody. *How beautiful*, she thought, but no one could play as well as Papa. Caliber's ears perked up. He heard it, too, and he glanced up at Scarlett-Rain.

Of course, it was illogical, but she felt a stab of guilt for being drawn to a stranger's music. Up until then, Papa's banjo was the only instrument that had filled her soul with joy. *How dare this stranger come along and disrupt that familiar safety with a charming brown song!*

Mama was still waiting by the wagon, but she didn't notice her daughter's enchanted, doe-like gaze staring out into the bustling street.

"Alright," Pleasant agreed at last. "You can wait in the wagon, but we're gonna have lunch together at that little inn." She pointed to a simple white building across the street. There was a long line of strange folks stretching out the open door, and Scarlett-Rain swallowed. The guitar music hummed away in the distance, changing to more of a happy yellowish-brown.

"Mama, why's there so many folks here?" In the many years she'd been visiting Calliway, she'd never seen so many people gathered together all at once.

Pleasant wrinkled her freckled nose. "Gold fever, Honey. Remember?"

Shaking her head, Mama made her way toward the mercantile, leaving Caliber sitting beside the wagon. He was staring into the crowd, with his gray ears erect, as he searched for the captivating tune. Climbing down from her seat, Scarlett-Rain hugged her fuzzy wolf. "Come on, ol' boy," she said as she stood. "Let's go find out who Papa's rival is."

CHAPTER FIVE

Love's First Touch

When Scarlett-Rain first laid eyes upon Johnathon Rucker, her soft heart pretended to die inside her chest, and for a frightening moment, she believed it. Without breathing, she instinctively clutched the fabric above her breastbone as she watched the guitar player. *Thump. Thump. S*he gasped, relieved to know life still flowed through her veins.

The simple truth was Johnathon Rucker could play his instrument better than Papa, and it pained Scarlett-Rain to admit it. With a deep, passionate voice, he spun a mesmerizing tale about a struggling coal miner as his fingers plucked away on old guitar strings. The young man wasn't naturally handsome, and his nose was slightly too large for his angular face. Like Papa, he was covered in the dark mark of coal, and it was easy to mistake him for a lean black man. However, Scarlett-Rain knew better. Beneath all that dirty grime was a seventeen-year-old boy with unevenly tanned skin and dark, coffee-colored eyes. His short hair was brown, matching his guitar, and a beaver-skin hat was cocked atop his head. His pants were tattered and patched, and a fur-lined coat gave the illusion that the boy was top-heavy and broad-shouldered (which was far from the truth).

Somehow, he didn't mind the small crowd that had gathered in front of the blacksmith's shop to watch him play. *Did he even notice them?* He was completely absorbed in his song, and Scarlett-Rain got the feeling his instrument was not an object at all but a friend with the same voice as Caliber and Papa's land.

With something like a silent, internal squeal, Scarlett-Rain observed the boy, in awe, from behind the protection of a water trough. Her bushy, black head peeped above the hiding place and strained to gaze at him between large breaks within the onlookers. For the first time in her life, Scarlett-Rain was smitten, and her heart fluttered like a feverish butterfly. He could have been the ugliest poor soul in Tennessee, and she wouldn't have noticed. Her hazel eyes saw perfection, and his love for that beaten-down, scuffed guitar worked magic tricks on her blushing cheeks. *Heavens to Betsy, he understood music!* All at once, like when God released every drop of moisture from the heavens in a gargantuan downpour, Scarlett-Rain loved the man.

Suddenly, she caught a glimpse of a red-headed girl standing next to the musician. Out of nowhere, the girl leaned over and planted a short kiss on his cheek. Scarlett-Rain recognized the girl from church. Her name was Sally Cotton. She was sixteen years old with buck teeth and freckles. Her lips were pink and plump, the perfect size to hide her teeth. Two long braids draped down her back. Rumors over the years claimed she was the prettiest gal in Calliway, but Scarlett-Rain didn't believe such nonsense. Miss Cotton was a gossip, and nosier than any female she'd ever met. She had an amazing talent for talking folks' ears off, yet not saying anything at all. She was popular, though, and Mama had once described her as "charming."

With force matching a tornado, painful anger whirled against Scarlett-Rain's unsuspecting tummy. Sally Cotton might have been the most popular girl in town, but she didn't understand music. No matter how hard she tried, Sally would never be able to see the colors Scarlett-Rain saw when the musician plucked his strings.

With a dry gulp, Scarlett-Rain reached over for Caliber and accidentally grabbed a lock of his fur. A wolfish howl broke through the musical air as he yelped in pain. Swiftly, the crowd turned to face the trough, and to her horror, Scarlett-Rain locked eyes with the melodic coal miner who had made her heart stop beating. His eyes seemed so sorrowful in that moment—*deep and trusting, even wild like the forest itself.*

Panicking, she tried to hoist herself up by grasping the trough, but clumsily, her boot slipped causing her upper body to plunge into the cold liquid. With a loud, girlish gasp, she emerged from the drinking water and backed away in both fear and embarrassment. Caliber was barking at the crowd for no good reason, and Scarlett-Rain clutched Mama's soaked dress. Sally Cotton was laughing at her awkward stunt, and many of the onlookers chuckled. The guitar player, however, was silent as he watched. *Did he pity her? Was he angry the blasted wolf ruined his song?*

In a daze, Scarlett-Rain backed away and tripped over the clinging, yellow gown. Stinging tears stuck to her cheeks, and she ran like a timid rabbit. Humiliation stuck to her insides like thick molasses. Foolishness was the worst emotion she'd ever felt, and it grabbed hold of her with as much ease as a fearsome giant.

Caliber followed his master all the way to the porch of the little, white inn where she stopped to wait for Mama. The line of dusty pioneers and miners, stricken with gold fever, still stretched out the door and far across the wide dirt road in the middle of the town. Several of the strangers stared wide-eyed at Scarlett-Rain as she sobbed against the building's whitewashed wood siding.

Her wet hair, which Mama had lovingly brushed earlier that morning, was wild and frizzy again. Caliber moaned and licked her boots. "*It's okay, ol' girl,*" he seemed to say over and over, but Scarlett-Rain ignored him. After all, even though he was a dog, he was still a *boy* (which meant he was clueless to delicate female reactions), and Scarlett-Rain didn't want to even think about the male species at that moment.

Full of self-pity, she hardly noticed when Johnathon Rucker touched her for the first time. It was a gentle touch, barely more noticeable than the fingers of a crisp breeze. When she turned around, she choked on her own salty spit, and gravity spun out of control. The guitar player was standing before her, and he was, at least, a foot taller. His awkward, blackened face morphed into a goofy grin revealing straight, yet slightly yellowed, teeth. Up close, his acorn-colored eyes held gray flecks of dew, like droplets from a woodland spring. His instrument was strapped across his back with a leather strap, and it peeked at Scarlett-Rain like a shy, little boy.

"Miss, are ya alrite?"

The man spoke in a rough, Southern accent, and the strong smells of sweat and coal blew against Scarlett-Rain's little nose. She fought to nod, but the disease of shyness roared with extreme intensity. Her pale cheeks turned sunset red, and she just blinked at him with her large, circular eyes.

Blast! He knows! The secret of her timidity was out, and she thought she glanced pity behind the boy's kind, twitching lips.

With an uncomfortable cough, he tipped his beaver hat and pointed at a piece of paper hanging behind Scarlett-Rain's head. Patches of light brown stubble stuck out from the black soot covering his bony chin and strong jaw. *Look away from his face!* Scarlett-Rain thought to herself. *Look away from his face!*

After an unnaturally long minute of staring at his features, the girl turned to the paper he was referring to. In bold, straight letters, the poster read:

CALLIWAY FAIR, THIS SATURDAY. COME ONE, COME ALL.

The boy shuffled his heavy boots, and Caliber growled silently at his movement.

"I'll be playin' then," the young man said. He studied the girl's red, tear-stained face and dripping dress. Out of nowhere, he reached out a shaky hand (which Scarlett-Rain thought was odd considering he was a guitar player) and gently stroked the tears from her girlish cheeks. Goosebumps soared across her satin skin, and the boy laughed.

"Great, now I just covered yer face in coal."

Trembling, Scarlett-Rain gave a weak smile and reached up to touch the place where his hand had been. *His hands...fingers that were strong enough to wield a pickaxe, yet graceful enough to pluck a guitar.* She didn't dare meet his gaze, and Caliber would not stop making that ridiculous, low growling noise. The boy raised his eyebrows at the dog.

"I'm Johnathon Rucker," he said finally as he stretched out a dark hand to Scarlett Rain. "You can call me Chief, though. Everybody else does."

Amazingly, she managed to nod in his presence—this boy who she loved, this coal miner who, no doubt preferred red-headed girls with buck teeth.

Quivering, she put her tiny hand inside his dirty palm. "Scarlett-Rain," she heard herself say, and Caliber barked like a cranky grandfather. "S-Scarlett-Rain M-Manchester."

Chief's eyes widened. "Manchester, did ya say?" He slapped his thigh as the wolf grunted. "Well, I'll be darned! I work with yer paw!"

Somehow, she dared to peek into his chocolate eyes but quickly looked away. Chief was grinning again, and she couldn't imagine why.

"Yer daddy's a right fine man," he said. "Quiet, like you, Miss, but tough as a bull."

Her cheeks reddened again, and she immediately crossed her skinny, wet arms, unsure how to hold them in his presence. Chief continued talking.

"I just settled here a few weeks ago. Folks say thar's gold in this territory, and I don't plan on missin' none of it."

The tornado hit Scarlett-Rain's stomach again. *So, he had the fever. Maybe that's why he favored silly, flirtatious girls like Sally Cotton.* She bit her pink lip and looked away from him, suddenly feeling ugly and vulnerable. Chief was staring at her, as if hoping she would speak, but she didn't. Caliber, at least, was pleased with her silence.

Chief rubbed the back of his neck. "I saw ya watchin' me play back thar." He shrugged. "I ain't too good, but I heard yer paw is somethin' of a fingerpickin' legend."

Amazingly, at the mention of Papa, Scarlett-Rain's dry lips moved, and words emerged. "Papa's the best banjo player in the whole darn territory," she said. *Why did she sound so defensive? Just shut up!* she told herself.

Chief laughed a happy tune, and she could feel his voice tickling her forehead.

"Of course, he is!" he agreed with a respectful bow. "Daughters do know best, after all."

He didn't believe her, and *was that a hint of arrogance in his tone?* It wasn't possible, but her heart tripped inside her chest as it fell in love all over again. *Was it even natural to fall in love multiple times with the same person?* Caliber was watching her reactions to the strange coal miner, and he was not the least bit amused. His wolf belly made that weird rumbling noise again.

Tell the boy you loved hearing him play, Scarlett-Rain demanded to herself. *Tell him you loved his music. Tell him now!*

Chief gave her an innocent, wrinkly grin as he scratched the back of his neck again. Across the street, Scarlett-Rain glimpsed Pleasant as she emerged from the mercantile. Their eyes locked for a moment, and Mama crossed her arms with a humorous, motherly smile.

"Uh...my mama's waitin' fer me," Scarlett-Rain said to Chief. He turned to follow her gaze and saw Mrs. Manchester waving at them across the road. Without a thought, he raised his strong, dirty hand and waved back to her. Even this small gesture from him was handsome to Scarlett-Rain, and she supposed she'd gone loony.

"Well, I gotta git back ter work," Chief said as he turned again to the girl. *Did he mean he had to go back to the mines? What kind of a boy goes to town and gets kisses from Sally Cotton during his work break?* For some reason, Scarlett-Rain felt her stomach knotting.

"Will I be seein' ya at the fair?" he dared to ask as he nodded toward the poster again.

Scarlett-Rain shook her head. "I don't go much to those things," she heard herself say, and she felt like punching herself in the nose. Caliber laughed at the man's gloomy expression.

"Well, ya should," Chief mumbled as he looked into her eyes.

Suddenly, his young, black face lit up with child-like enthusiasm. "Hey, I know!" he said as he snapped his tough fingers. "I'll ask yer paw if I can take ya thar myself!"

Caliber moaned in pain, and Scarlett-Rain nudged him with her boot. Chief was staring at her with his huge, yellow-tinted grin as if waiting for a reply, so she nodded.

"Alritey then," he breathed in relief, and for a long moment, they just stood there hovering beside each other.

Pleasant was pretending not to watch them from across the street, but there was only a limited amount of time a woman could stare into a shop window without looking like an attractive thief. Chief gave Scarlett-Rain a swift nod with his fuzzy beaver cap.

"Well, until Saturday, Miss Scarlett-Rain."

Chuckling, he walked away and began to sing an old song. Somewhere down the road, Sally Cotton was searching for her wandering musician. Johnathon avoided her, or perhaps he didn't see her. Scarlett-Rain wasn't sure, but when Mama came to fetch her, Scarlett-Rain's feminine eyes, like gold-dusted timbers, were glossed over with newfound womanhood. Caliber pouted and howled, but Mama just smiled. Trembling, Scarlett-Rain reached up to touch the coal smudges on her cheeks.

CHAPTER SIX

Echo in the Wilderness

As the Manchesters' wagon rolled across Papa's land, Scarlett-Rain hopped out to head for the nearby lookout. She needed to think, and Mama's girlish interrogations about Chief were enough to drive any new woman mad. "He's a nice lad," Pleasant had said during their mother-daughter lunch at the inn. "We've gotta invite that boy ter supper soon. I'll talk ta Papa about it this evenin'." However, Mama's fascination with the guitar player didn't end at lunchtime. On the long ride home, her questions about the musical coal miner came in pairs of two and sometimes three.

"Mama, I only just met the boy!" Scarlett-Rain had told her. She didn't dare mention the dark truth about Johnathon Rucker's fever. Besides, it was probably just a *touch* of temperature, she reasoned with herself. It would pass soon enough.

Nevertheless, Mama was smitten with the idea of having a coal miner for a son-in-law, and Scarlett-Rain's nerves swirled anxiously within her tummy. When the girl jumped out of the wagon, Pleasant just sighed and let her go. Caliber leaped after her, and to Scarlett-Rain's delight, the wilderness was still angry at her for the crime of growing up. There would be silence at the lookout today, and she craved the quiet.

She wasn't sure how long she lay on that giant rock that was jutting into the abyss. The midday sun splattered across her cheeks, and for a while, she forgot about the cool September air. Caliber was sprawled out on the back part of the rock, closer to the safety of the ground, and Scarlett-Rain huffed at his cowardice.

The presence of love was everywhere Scarlett-Rain looked, and if she squinted hard enough, she could see the black painting of Chief in the shadows of the clouds.

He had a cute smile—cute and imperfect. What more could a girl want? She laughed aloud to herself, dizzy with this exotic new feeling. *He liked her! He actually liked her!* Her eyebrows raised, and she reached her skinny arms toward Johnathon Rucker's picture in the sky. After taking a quick peek at the napping wolf, she scrunched her pink lips together and struggled to make an alluring kissing face.

Suddenly, a high-pitched laugh broke the silence, and Scarlett-Rain bolted upright with heated embarrassment. "Who is thar?" she demanded as the breeze grabbed her wild hair. Caliber immediately jumped from his sleep, and a bronze bush rustled nearby.

"Quit spyin' on me!" Scarlett-Rain yelled to the intruder, and before she could continue her scolding, a little girl with short, canary pigtails stepped into view. She was a tiny, pitiful thing with a crusty, old dress and apron that seemed to swallow her whole. Her skin was brown from frequent rendezvous with the sun, and her vanilla bonnet was dangling from the back of her neck. Almost instantly, she giggled and stuck her tongue out at Scarlett-Rain.

"Echo Springfield!" Scarlett-Rain hollered. She eyed her closest neighbor and church acquaintance with a scowl. It was hard to believe the little mouse was thirteen.

Laughing, Echo made a dramatic kissy-face toward the clouds. "You're dumb," she said bluntly to Scarlett-Rain, and her wrinkled, youthful face, like leather, was pinched in disgust. "Kissin' is gross."

"Well, how would *you* know?" Scarlett-Rain retorted. "You ain't nevva even done it befur!"

Echo crossed her bony arms. "I've seen my three brothers kissin' girls befur, when they thought nobody was lookin', and trust me, it's yucky!"

Scarlett-Rain rolled her big eyes. The thought of the giant, smelly Springfield boys swapping spit with dainty females made her cringe. "Yer brothers ain't nothin' but a bunch of sloppy pack-mules!" she declared, and Echo just snorted in agreement.

"So, who *were* ya dreamin' about kissin'?" she asked.

Scarlett-Rain gasped. "Nunna ya business, Springfield!"

Echo clasped her hands behind her back as she stepped closer to her neighbor. Her crystal-blue eyes were gleaming in the high sun, and Caliber let out a low, rumbling growl as leaves cracked beneath the girl's old boots.

"Does he work with our papas perhaps?" Echo guessed with witch-like intuition. Sometimes, Scarlett-Rain forgot that Willy Springfield, Echo's daddy, was a coal miner, too. According to Dillon, the man was lazy and careless with his work, but Papa was too kind to complain much about Echo's father. "It's just how some folks are," he'd say, "but the Lord will reward those of us who have callused hands."

Scarlett-Rain rolled out her bottom lip. "Yer a witch," she said, repeating what the wilderness had always told her about the Springfields.

"What? Yer crazy!" Echo gawked, and Caliber laughed in dog-like agreement with his master.

For a long moment, the three of them stood together, awkwardly, in the burgundy September breeze. Papa's land was still silent, and Scarlett-Rain wanted nothing more than to yank Echo's nosy ponytails.

"Hey, I know!" Willy's daughter said, at last. "Let's go down ter the mines, so I can see this fella you've gone crossed-eyed over!"

Caliber barked in protest, and Scarlett-Rain shook her head.

"No!"

Papa always warned her never to go down to the mines without his permission. It was a dangerous place not fit for the eyes of little girls. However, Scarlett-Rain was a brand-new woman now. *Did that silly, childish rule still apply?*

Echo's rebellious smile was devilish, and Scarlett-Rain didn't trust it at all.

"Alright," she agreed with a groan, "but if I git a whippin', yer gittin' one with me!"

Not waiting to hear anymore, Echo was off, pigtails flying. "Race ya, dumb-brain!" she called out, and Scarlett-Rain had no choice but to follow. Caliber was bounding behind them, yelping like a distraught grandpa. Electric adrenaline coursed through Scarlett-Rain's veins as she imagined Chief's black, prickly face. *Oh, how she loved him!* She could feel her heart's smile stretching the limits of her small chest. *She wouldn't be caught spying on him this time! No sir!* She would look upon her love, in peace, as he worked, and who cared about the unwanted company of Caliber and Echo? Chief was all that mattered. His song was all she could hear.

As they ran through the forest, a soft cry whistled through the butterscotch pines. *"Come back, Scarlett-Rain. You'll forget us. Come back."*

CHAPTER SEVEN

The Mines

The ground rumbled as Scarlett-Rain, Echo and Caliber neared the hill overlooking the mines. Pleasant was always fretting and crying about her husband working with explosives, and many times, Scarlett-Rain had seen Mama crumble with fear on the cabin floor when the land shook with the same ferocity as a dragon's roar. "What's that noise, Mama?" Scarlett-Rain would ask, and Pleasant would sniff. "Just the mines fightin' back, Honey. Don't ya worry, now! Papa will be alrite! He knows what he's doin'!" Silently sobbing, Mama would start washing dishes with her own tears.

Caliber howled at the quaking ground, and Echo fell, face first, in the tall grass. With a scream, Scarlett-Rain tripped over her neighbor.

"Whooooooa!" Echo yelled at the explosion with weird delight. "Thar really *is* a beast inside them darn caves! I always knew my daddy was a knight!"

Scarlett-Rain rolled her eyes while pulling leaves out of her tangled hair. "You really are a child," she said as she stood. With shaking legs, she approached the edge of the hill and crouched low to get a good view of the caverns down below. The mines' main entrance was a large, gaping, black hole filled with flecks of lantern light. For a breathless moment, Scarlett-Rain imagined that big, open mouth really did hold a dragon somewhere deep inside, and it was waiting patiently to devour mighty prey. Dozens of menfolk, dark and dusty, were going in and out of the nearest tunnel, and Scarlett-Rain spotted Papa almost instantly.

He was bent over a water barrel, and he sucked the cool liquid from his tin cup like a sloppy bear. With a deep sigh, he scooped up more water to pour over his head and chest, then wiped his mouth with his dirty hand. The September sun pressed heavily upon the gorge below, and though it was a crisp, perfect day, the coal miners reeked with the sweat of July.

Caliber and Echo crawled over to Scarlett-Rain, like soldiers creeping through a thicket. To the shock of both Caliber and his master, Echo cursed. "Agh! My pa's drinkin' his potion again!"

Immediately, Scarlett-Rain threw her hand over the child's lips. "Shut up!" she demanded. "Do ya want 'em ter catch us?" She stared into her neighbor's pale blue eyes, like diamonds on waves of sea-foam. Caliber groaned with sensitive discomfort of being so close to the dragon's mouth. Scarlett-Rain grunted. "You two is the worst soldiers ever! Yer endangerin' the mission!" She pulled back Echo's messy, yellow bangs to gaze hard into her rough face. "And no cussin' ever again, Springfield! Golly, didn't yer pa evva teach ya better than that?"

Echo just shrugged as Scarlett-Rain released her face.

"My paw says those words all the time," said Echo, "especially when he's angry."

Scarlett-Rain opened her mouth to speak but blushed instead. It was obvious to everyone in the county that the Springfields' homelife was a whirlwind, but *what was she supposed to say to the girl?* Out of nowhere, Caliber started grooming Echo's arm with his sandpaper tongue.

Cheeks still burning, Scarlett-Rain turned to look down at Papa again. Echo's father, Willy, was several feet away from him. Like most of the miners, Mr. Springfield was wiping sweat from his forehead, only he wasn't working. He was lounging on a rock with a whiskey jug in one hand.

A young man wearing a beaver hat stepped up to Dillon and slapped him kindly on his iron shoulders. His skin and clothes were covered in the dragon's black spit, but Scarlett-Rain could recognize him anywhere. Though the air was comfortably cool, she froze on top of the hill, and her legs jerked with a strange, hilarious spasm. Echo snorted.

"So, that's him," Springfield said, unimpressed, as her ocean eyes flickered down upon Chief. "He shore is an ugly son-of-a-gun."

For a frightening moment, Johnathon Rucker's chestnut eyes grazed the top of the ledge where the young soldiers were hiding. Scarlett-Rain nearly swallowed her tongue as she jumped to press down Echo and Caliber's heads. *Did Chief just grin?* Papa was rambling and pointing inside the mouth of the closest cave, and though Chief appeared to be listening, Scarlett-Rain knew he wasn't. Somehow, he was up on that hill, too, and she could feel his laughing, ghostly presence.

With cheeks as red as the month of June, Scarlett-Rain gazed down at her love. *Who cared if he was drenched in sweat and grime? He was beautiful.* Warm chills suddenly dotted across her skin, beneath the fine hairs on her arms. Somehow, she knew this memory would be forever tattooed within her daytime dreams. Behind her sleeping eyelids, a black warrior, wielding an old guitar and pickaxe, would protect her from nightmare's shadows.

"You've got it bad," Echo whispered while staring at Scarlett-Rain's bewitched, pale face. "What's that ugly, ol' boy doin' here in this territory anyway?"

"He ain't ugly!" Scarlett-Rain hissed. "He's...lovely..."

Chief, not-so-casually, stretched his arms and back as he spoke with Dillon. Even the beaming sun seemed to favor that teenage coal miner who understood music better than anyone in the territory. *Did Papa know he was conversing with his rival?*

"He's got the fever," Scarlett-Rain heard herself whisper. "My love has the fever..."

Echo wrinkled her leather nose. "What? He's sick?"

"Yes...he's got gold fever."

For a long while, the three of them gazed down upon the diseased guitar player. Dillon seemed oblivious to the musical truth that was Johnathon Rucker, and he was certainly still unaware of that wiry lad's intentions to escort his only daughter to a public fair. If Scarlett-Rain peered close enough, she could see a gentle smile behind Papa's stern, steel-set jaw. *He approved of Chief, his natural-born enemy—the very man that would one day steal his daughter and take his place. Poor Papa...for perhaps the first time in his life, Dillon Manchester was clueless.*

"They's only one way ter cure gold fever," Echo said while blinking her large, sky-blue eyes.

"How?" asked Scarlett-Rain, and Caliber snorted with doggish displeasure.

"We've got ter find the gold," said Springfield. "We've gotta find it befur all them new settlers find it. We've got ter find it and give it ter yer boy. Only then will his itchin' fever subside."

"I don't know," said Scarlett-Rain. "That sounds purty stupid."

The wolf whined in agreement with his master.

"Ya wanna marry that ugly ol' boy one day, don'tcha?" whispered Echo.

"Yeah."

"Then ya gotta give him what he wants. He wants gold."

Caliber cried a little too loudly, and Scarlett-Rain scolded him. Perhaps the scrawny, yellow-feathered bird called Echo was right. Maybe gold *was* the only way to buy Chief. Scarlett-Rain remembered Papa warning her to stay away from folks sick with the fever. A misty plan began to form inside her head. If she could cure Chief of his illness, then all her dreams would come true. *Johnathon would be well again, and no one would know of his sins.*

Scarlett-Rain squinted hard at Echo. "Alright, crazy soldier."

Echo grinned with impish magnitude. "Come on then. Let's start huntin'."

CHAPTER EIGHT

Papa's Supper Guest

All day, the sun danced across the wild Tennessee skies, and Scarlett-Rain and Caliber trailed along behind Echo, like brave explorers searching for the wilderness's brightest secrets. It wasn't long before Willy's daughter found what she deemed a "sweet spot" within one of Papa's rivers, and the two girls splashed and hooted, like Indians, as the wolf watched with kinglike pride upon a soggy bank close by.

"We'll shore find the gold here!" Echo promised as she scooped up piles of mud from the shallow river bottom with her apron. "We'll call this water *Chieftain's Drink,* because this is the river that's hidin' Rucker's cure! Tomorrow, I'll bring some sifters. That's how them settlers do it. I seen 'em."

Scarlett-Rain sighed. Though Springfield was deaf to its cry, the river wailed, like a giant baby, with every poke and prod to its ancient dirt. *"Those are my pebbles, you little witch!"* it hissed and raged. *"That's my mud!"*

At long last, the cool water appeared to rise in threatening vengeance, and Scarlett-Rain snapped at the stream's dangerous sensitivity.

"Would you shut up?" she yelled as she kicked the water. Mama's daisy-yellow dress was hiked up to her hip, revealing her long, slender legs—legs that still wobbled with girlhood but graced the promise of womanhood. Pleasant's best gown was sopping wet and muddied, yet again, and Scarlett-Rain's thick, charcoal hair was plastered all across her porcelain face.

Echo was staring at her companion with wise, blue eyes, like glittering marbles set against shaved buffalo hide.

"Are you cracked or somethin'?" the girl asked with a fair eyebrow arched against her forehead.

"I ain't no more cracked than you are," Scarlett-Rain shot back, embarrassed that someone caught her speaking to the river.

With a shrug, Springfield stuck out her raspberry tongue at her friend and kept digging.

With a gentle breath, the peach-colored hours of the autumn afternoon soon melted into colder rays of pale sapphire twilight. Caliber and Scarlett-Rain made the long trek back home along wagon-rut roads and shaded blue forests. Mama was waiting in the illuminated front door of the cabin. One hand was on her hip, and the other was gripping a wooden spoon. With a high-pitched, motherly voice, she fretted when she saw the soaked dress decorated with clumps of dried mud.

"You go wash out that gown this instant, young lady!" she demanded. With jungle eyes, like lightning, she pulled her daughter's sludge-splattered face up to meet her gaze. With a twitch of her narrow jaw, she said, "I'll go heat yer bathwater."

Saying nothing, Scarlett-Rain did as she was told. She knew better than to back-talk Mama. Pleasant might have been dainty and thin, but she could thaw even the fastest gunslinger out West with her shattered stare. Mostly, she was joyful and bright, like a bluebird in May, but when she was unhappy, the spell of an enchantress would come over her freckled face. It was impossible to break her heart, because she always got her way. Laughing, Papa would call that look, "a woman's charm" (or something like that).

So, feeling childishly guilty for her romp in *Chieftain's Drink*, Scarlett-Rain cleaned Mama's soft dandelion dress in the washtub behind the house. When she was finished, she hung the gown on the clothesline to dry and went back inside the cabin.

Pleasant was waiting for her, in the middle of the room, beside a big, round bucket of steaming bathwater. Caliber was already asleep, ears twitching, in his stinking corner. Growling and grunting, he moved his legs rapidly as invisible, bushy-tailed foxes eluded him.

Scarlett-Rain stripped off her stained undergarments and stepped into the bin. For the next several minutes, Mama scrubbed her with a rough brush and said nothing. It wasn't long before Dillon's deep singing voice came flowing through the tiny cracks between the log walls.

"Meet me by the moonlight, Darlin', meet me.
Meet me by the moonlight tonight, tonight.
I have a sad story to tell you,
beneath the sweet moonlight, tonight."
"Papa's home!"

Caliber bolted from his sleep and leaped for the door as bits of slate-gray fur flew through the air. Quickly, Pleasant tossed a plush towel to her daughter, and Scarlett-Rain grabbed it.

Somewhere, across the distance, another soothing voice rang out with Papa's, and Scarlett-Rain fell, stark naked, out of the bucket with a loud plop on the hardwood floor.

"Goodness gracious," Pleasant squealed as she helped her daughter stand. "What's gotten inta you, Baby?"

Scarlett-Rain's hazel eyes clung wide and desperate to the rose curtain covering the front window. Papa wasn't alone tonight, and the voice that accompanied him was none other than the brown, strong melody of his rival, Chief.

"I have a ship sailin' on the ocean,
burdened with silver and gold,
and before my sweetheart should suffer,
I'd have the ship anchored and sold.
If I had wings like an angel,
over these prison bars, I would fly.
I'd fly to the arms of my darlin'.
With her, I'd be willin' to die."

"I-It's h-him!" Scarlett-Rain managed to squeak as she pressed the towel against her sopping chest. Mama's fern eyes danced back and forth with hidden rush and merriment. Failing to hide her pinkish smile, she looked at her daughter.

"Hurry!" she said. "Go upstairs and fetch my old pink dress outta the wood chest! It oughtta fit!"

Breathless, they stared at each other, and Mama understood. She could see the fear and love within her child's grayish-green eyes, like tree bark on a foggy spring morning. She knew Scarlett-Rain was in love. It was a truth impossible to hide. A stray tear slipped down Pleasant's grin.

"It's gonna be alrite, Honey," she said as she cupped her callused hands beneath her daughter's chin. Then a giggle escaped her spotted, regal face, still full of youth's eternal dance.

"That boy likes you!"

Caliber howled as he stood before the door, and Scarlett-Rain playfully slapped at Mama.

After drying off, Scarlett-Rain sprinted for the ladder leading to the loft. Clumsily, she clambered up the steps praying Johnathon and Papa wouldn't bust through the front door and behold her naked bottom. *Ugh!* She almost died just imagining it!

Mama's pink dress was stored away in a large, wooden chest, along with other old clothes. Pleasant rarely got rid of fabric, no matter how worn. Everything could be reused. Scarlett-Rain opened the heavy lid and pulled out the gown. Quickly, she slid it over her shoulders. The hem was too long, and the material bunched on the floor beside her feet. The sleeves were lacy and constricting on the ends, and a button was missing along the neckline. She sighed. *Why did she have to follow that brainless Echo into that miserable creek? If only she hadn't soiled Mama's pretty yellow gown! Blast that Echo!*

After attempting to adjust the dress, she heard the downstairs door open, and Papa's booming, "hello, Darlin!" nearly shook the cabin with its bliss. She could almost hear the honey-pink kiss he gave to Mama with his dusted, salty mouth. Caliber was growling and barking, worse than a perturbed clown, at the other man who entered the house, no doubt. All at once, Chief's cedar-colored voice spilled across Scarlett-Rain's skin, like warm pecan syrup. "Howdy, Ma'am," he said to Pleasant, and Scarlett-Rain watched her own cheeks turn a violent shade of red in the vanity mirror.

Quietly, she threw herself against the edge of the loft's floor and peered down below at the main room. Caliber was drooling at the mouth, circling around Johnathon's boots, like a wild beast plagued with rabies.

Papa scolded the animal and nudged him away with his leg. Pouting, the wolf-dog ran to his putrid corner to sulk in his own spit.

To Scarlett-Rain's horror, Chief's beaver hat tilted upward toward the loft, and his umber eyes caught her hazel stare. Immediately, he gave her an offset grin, and she just lay there, on her stomach, as her legs turned into liquid jelly.

"Where's Scarlett-Rain?" Papa asked Mama, and their daughter yanked herself away from the edge of the loft. After a silent prayer to God, she tugged at her scratchy sleeves and began climbing down the ladder. Never before, in her fifteen years of life, had she felt so hideous and vulnerable. *Scrawny limbs...an old gown that was too long...wild, tangled hair...what could Chief possibly have been smiling about?*

When she reached the bottom of the steps, she turned to face them all with glowing cheeks. Johnathon's toothy grin was still cocked to the side of his blackened face, and Scarlett-Rain wondered if she'd ever see him without the mask of coal. Like Papa, Chief wore soot like a comfortable second layer of skin.

Dillon cleared his throat. "Johnathon, this is my baby girl, Scarlett-Rain. Scarlett-Rain, this is Johnathon

Rucker—new feller down at the mines." Papa nodded to Mama. "Of course, this is my wife, Pleasant."

Chief tipped his hat to both of the ladies. "Nice ter meet y'all—again," he said with ease and simple grace. Then he gave a wink to Scarlett-Rain.

"I met yer daughter in town today," he continued to Papa. "She was kind enough ta help some horses get a drink of water, I believe."

Was he teasing her? Scarlett-Rain didn't know whether to giggle or fly back up the ladder. Mama laughed, like wind chimes in a dew-sprinkled breeze.

"Why don'tcha come sit down fer supper with us, Johnathon?" Pleasant said, smiling as she walked away to prepare the table.

Chief removed his sweaty hat, and Scarlett-Rain tried not to stare at his dark walnut hair, sticking out in every direction. "Why, I'd be much obliged, Ma'am," he said politely. Still peeking at Scarlett-Rain, he followed Papa to a maple washstand on the opposite side of the room. Shuffling his boots, he waited for Dillon to clean his arms and face and then he followed suit.

Without breathing, Scarlett-Rain floated to the supper table to help Mama. Pleasant had already set out the flowery blue and white plates (the finest ones they owned), so together, they filled the dishes with hot corn muffins, sweet potatoes, lima beans and turkey. Black coffee was poured into Papa and Chief's tin cups, and the ladies had fresh, cool water.

Papa sat in his usual place at the head of the table, and Mama faced him on the opposite end. Their daughter and Chief were seated on the left and right sides, and Scarlett Rain couldn't imagine which would have been the better scenario: facing Johnathon all throughout dinner or sitting alongside him. Ultimately, she decided that eating beside him would have been better, because at least, there would have been a reason to avoid eye contact. Nevertheless, to her shy horror, he sat opposite her, giving him the freedom to stare as much as he wanted. She, on the other hand, was not bold enough to gaze upon him in front of her parents. As she looked at her bread, she wondered if, perhaps, she would forget how to chew and swallow.

"So, where ya from, Johnathon?" Mama asked after a bite of sweet corn muffin.

Scarlett-Rain's timid eyes, like a young doe, snatched a quick glimpse at Chief's rough features, and all at once, she felt the burning of her heart fall in love again. Wondrously, the water basin had performed some miracle, because Johnathon's tan, prickly face was now fresh and untouched by grime. He had a jagged face, resilient and austere, like a young mountain, but there was summer laughter there and even sorrow shaped like a martin bird's song.

"I'm from down south of here," Chief replied to Pleasant, "all over really. I was born in Alabama. That's where my folks live—what's left of 'em anyways."

Pleasant took a swallow of her drink. "And what brings ya ta Tennessee?" she asked with too much interest, and Scarlett-Rain cringed.

"Gold," he replied through a mouthful of turkey. Mama and Papa glanced at each other.

"Fool's errand," Dillon said bluntly as he chewed. "Yer too young and too valuable ter go wastin' yer life away chasin' the devil's riches."

Chief laughed good-heartedly.

"You don't understand, Sir," he said kindly. "I've always had nothin'—not a penny ter my name, but...ter find *gold*...why, a man could die happy with that kinda luck."

Dillon was quiet for several minutes as he ate his beans. Then he looked up and nodded toward Chief's guitar propped beside the front door. "You call that *nothin'*," he said simply.

Johnathon was silent, and Dillon continued.

"I hear the boys at work callin' ya *Chief*. They say ya can play music louder and purtier than an injun chief's mighty war cry." He looked at his young rival. "Is they right?"

To Scarlett-Rain's surprise, Johnathon just shrugged while staring at his plate.

"They *is* right, Papa!" Scarlett-Rain heard herself shout. "I heard him play, and he's the best—I mean..."

Instantly, red blotches seized her face again. Mama was holding back a smile, and Papa raised his eyebrows, almost humorously.

"Well," Dillon said as he wiped his big hands on his pants. "They's only one way ter settle this argument."

His chair scraped across the floor as he stood to go grab Rucker's guitar. With a gleam in his eye, he also grabbed his own banjo, next to the fireplace, and returned to his seat. Papa's lips formed a straight line across his square face. "Well, Chief," he said as he handed him the guitar. "No one's bested me, yet."

CHAPTER NINE

The Duel

The music started off slow, and Scarlett-Rain watched Papa's fingers dance across the banjo strings in the firelight. His eyes were not focused on his instrument but on Chief, instead. The song Papa played was as natural as breathing, and Johnathon's guitar was silent below its master's slouched shoulders. The banjo whined as it began a sad tale of love. The tune was quiet and sure of itself—steady as the oldest rock planted by the flightiest of rivers. Papa was confident of this song—this story he had sung with unsurpassed passion since the day his daughter was born.

Chief didn't know the song or the melody. How could he? No one but Papa could play this tune, and this secret fact filled Dillon with warm pride. As a huge grin spread across his grizzly bear face, Papa's fingers began to move a bit faster. Tawny chords dripping with hues of marigold and rust sang to Scarlett-Rain's delicate ears. The music was a whispering reminder of Papa's unconditional love —a song so sorrowful, its beauty was almost heartbreaking.

Out of nowhere, a loud, dominant "G" chord, soaked in shades of mocha and cider, disrupted Papa's graceful melody. Chief's guitar had joined the tale, and the banjo screamed like the symphony of a roaring wind. All at once, the two instruments ripped at each other in loud musical unison. The banjo fought, like a knight of old, to defend its sweet love story as the guitar battled to take its place. The ambience was wild and desperate as the cacophony of amber notes weaved together a complex masterpiece.

Scarlett-Rain wasn't sure how long the duel would rage on, but with every stroke of Papa and Chief's firm hands against the strings, she could feel her spirit splitting. This was no ordinary duet but a challenge of dominions, a clash of masters. Only one could claim victory in the end, and Scarlett-Rain was the prize.

There is a solemn, well-known fact about fatherhood (especially when it concerns daughters). Sooner or later, the old man must admit defeat to the young man. With quiet love and humility, a daddy must eventually give away his most precious gift to the lad who vanquishes him. It takes a special kind of man to allow himself to be conquered, and Dillon Manchester knew, from the first moment he heard his baby girl cry, what would one day be required of him.

Naturally, the hours pressed on into the darker corners of the night, and like the thousands of noble fathers before him, Scarlett-Rain's papa finally laid down his banjo. With tears in his heavy eyelids, he applauded his opponent and shook hands with a broken smile.

Mama was at the table, clapping with wet, star-filled eyes. She knew what had just occurred, and without hesitating, she walked over to her husband to plant a kiss within his black, winter-sprinkled hair. She whispered something to him, but Scarlett-Rain couldn't hear.

Dillon looked at Johnathon and said, "to everythin' there is a season... Congratulations, Chief. I now see that yer title is deserved."

Did Rucker just blush? Scarlett-Rain couldn't believe it. Not only had her true love bested Papa, but he was ashamed of his victory. He seemed sorry to have to cut the old man down. For a moment, Scarlett-Rain imagined Chief to be a young woodcutter, and her father was the toughest, mightiest oak tree in the wilderness. Johnathon hated to have to swing his axe at that majestic oak, but nature, itself, beckoned him to do it. Over, the giant tree fell with a loud crash, and the woodcutter was left standing there with a bent look of sorrow on his face.

Suddenly, all eyes were on Scarlett-Rain, and Mama spoke first. "Honey, why don't ya step outside with Chief for a few moments before he goes home?"

Immediately, Johnathon stood with his guitar strap still slung across his shoulder and chest. His jaw twitched as words spilled out of his mouth too quickly.

"I'm sorry I imposed on you folks like this," he said with modesty etched across his face, "especially you, Sir." He nodded to Dillon. "The food was mighty fine, and the company was even better." His gaze danced over to Scarlett-Rain's pale cheeks glowing in the firelight. "The truth is, I reckon I do have a favor ter task of you folks—if ya don't mind a feller bein' so bold, that is."

"What is it?" Mama asked too eagerly, and Papa was scratching the stubble on his chin.

Chief continued, "well, ya see, they's a fair this Saturday in Calliway, and I'd be mighty happy if I could escort yer daughter thar with me. I'll be playin' guitar thar, and I know she likes music."

Papa was as rigid as stone in his chair, and for a second, his chocolate eyes raced to the shotgun hanging on the mantle above the fireplace. Pleasant bit her lips, holding back a sweet smile, and Scarlett-Rain clutched her seat, fearful she might pass out on the floor. *Was she supposed to speak?* She hoped not, because her tongue was as limp as a dead fish.

Dillon crossed his enormous arms. "Alright," he said, at last. "I don't see the harm it would do." His black eyebrows narrowed at Chief. "You do know the rules, don'tcha, boy?"

Scarlett-Rain had no idea what Papa was talking about, but Johnathon understood. With a steady nod, he promised something invisible to Dillon.

"Yes, Sir."

Papa huffed at his reply. "My daughter's worth more ter me than all the gold in these fine hills, and I'll not give her up ter any cocky lad who thinks otherwise."

"Yes, Sir," Chief said, and Dillon grunted again.

For several long moments, they said nothing. Finally, Papa looked at Scarlett-Rain. "What do ya think, Baby Cake? Ya wanna go with this scruffy-haired coal miner?"

Chief chuckled with a boyish grin at Papa's words, and Scarlett-Rain nodded.

"Very well..." Dillon said while still staring at his daughter. "The maiden has decided."

Slowly, he stood from his chair and walked to open the front door for Johnathon. The hinges creaked as an unwelcome, chilly breeze entered the warm cabin. Mama motioned for Scarlett-Rain to follow Rucker out, and she did as she was told. After shaking hands with Chief, Papa closed the door, leaving his daughter alone, in the darkness, with her love.

It took her eyes several minutes to adjust to the blindness of night, but Scarlett-Rain could just make out the shadows of Chief's beaver hat below the winking stars. She could hear him smile, and she was thankful he couldn't witness her strawberry cheeks.

"We're gonna have fun Saturday," Johnathon said, and then he paused. "You don't go out in public much, do ya?"

Scarlett-Rain shrugged, which she realized was stupid because he couldn't see her.

Chief went on. "Oh, I don't like bein' in public either. It's just that...with you bein' so purty 'n all, I figured they'd be four or five fellas I'd have ter knock out ter even git a chance ter be with ya."

Scarlett-Rain's skin burned with girlish glee and embarrassment. *He called her pretty!* Before she realized it, her mouth started moving, and she couldn't be sure which words were barreling out.

"Well, dumb ol' Henry Springfield did try ter kiss me once, at church, when we was kids, but I punched his fat lips clear across the church pew before he evva tried that again! Papa said he nevva did see a female who could punch as fast as me!"

To her surprised delight, Chief burst out laughing, filling her senses with his familiar, brown song.

"Well, I'll have ta remember ter keep my lips ta myself—for a little while, at least."

Was that a question? Scarlett Rain didn't know how to respond, but the thought of his lips touching hers sent a wave of heat across the electric goosebumps on her arms.

"That's a purty dress, by the way," Johnathon said to the darkness, "but I like the yeller one best...the one ya were wearin' in town today...the one ya were wearin' at the mines this afternoon..."

The summer rush that was traveling across Scarlett-Rain's tiny body stopped with a jolt. Sweat dripped down her neck, despite the coldness of the air, and panic started to rise in unison with green humiliation. She could feel her throat constricting with shyness.

Chief shuffled his boots and continued. "So, what were ya doin' up on that hill?"

A tiny cloud of breath pushed itself out of Scarlett-Rain's lips. *What would she tell him? She couldn't admit the truth!* If Chief knew that she and Echo were there to spy on him, he'd probably think they were immature. She could feel her lifeless tongue swelling again as she tried, in desperation, to come up with an excuse—*any excuse.*

"The mines!" she squeaked in a pitch higher than that of a mouse. "Me and my friend—we w-wanted ter see the mines!"

Johnathon was silent in the blue-tinged darkness, and the edges of his beaver cap seemed lit with glowing moonlight.

"I see..." he said, at last. "After all, the mines are a lot more interestin' than spyin' on a feller ya secretly like."

The inside of Scarlett-Rain's mouth went completely numb as if a fierce wind had sucked away all signs of moisture.

"We was—I mean...the mines—we w-was..."

Johnathon let out another hearty laugh. "It's alright, Miss. Yer secret's safe with me."

Suddenly, deep inside Scarlett-Rain's heart, a provoked she-wolf leaped with defensive instinct. She could hardly believe what she said next, but it felt good to release it (even if she was trembling like a child).

"And I reckon yer guitar is a lot more interestin' than a kiss from *Sally Cotton!*"

Even though she couldn't see Rucker's face, Scarlett-Rain knew the she-wolf had hit her target with dangerous accuracy.

Chief was no longer laughing.

"How old are you?" he said simply.

"Fifteen. You?"

"...Seventeen."

Both of them waited as the silence attempted to strangle them together. Nearby, crickets played a sleepy song that was drenched in nighttime shades of cornflower blue. The tune gave Scarlett-Rain quiet peace.

"I'm sorry about what ya saw in front of the blacksmith's shop..." Chief said with a sigh, and Scarlett-Rain felt guilt's reliable sting. "I'd never met that gal befur that moment. She just walked up and kissed me... Will you ever forgive me?"

Scarlett-Rain shrugged again, though her love still couldn't see.

"Yer papa's shore right about one thang," Chief continued. "You really are the purtiest gal in the whole territory. A man would be a fool not ter see it."

Scarlett-Rain blushed so hard, it actually hurt—or maybe it was the nibbling cold. Without warning, Rucker reached up to lightly brush the side of her cheek in the darkness.

"If I see ya at the mines again," he said, "I won't tell. I'll pretend not ter notice ya."

Scarlett-Rain smiled, and she knew he could hear her lips parting.

"But if I do catch ya up on that hill again," he continued, "you've gotta promise ter wait fer me, and I'll come talk to ya on my lunch break."

Scarlett-Rain nodded as his callused fingers stroked her face again. Though his head was covered in shadow, she could feel Chief's coffee-scented breath hugging her nose with soft waves. He had moved in closer—too close, and she turned her head away.

Immediately, Papa knocked three times on the other side of the door, signaling it was time for Chief to leave.

"Where's yer house?" Scarlett-Rain asked quickly, and Johnathon chuckled.

"It ain't too far from here," he said, "but it ain't much of a home right now. There's no roof, ya see, and one of the walls is cavin' in. I bought it fer cheap when I settled out here a few weeks ago. It'll take me a while ter git the place livable again."

"You don't have a roof?" Scarlett-Rain said, incredulously. "Where do ya sleep when it rains?"

"Oh, I make do," Johnathon replied. "Besides, it does a person good to sleep beneath the stars."

Saying nothing, they both looked up into the twinkling abyss, and Papa rapped on the door again. With a tip of his beaver hat, Chief bade Scarlett-Rain goodnight and walked away, whistling to the darkness.

The universe seemed to crave Scarlett-Rain's attention, and she peered up into that mysterious black ocean for a long time. *"Gold,"* she whispered to herself, for the stars were tinted yellow, like tiny flecks of priceless treasure floating somewhere far beyond the outstretched arm of mankind. Maybe that's why Chief liked the stars so much—they reminded him of his dream, the very fever that ran wild within his veins.

Scarlett-Rain sighed. Echo's stupid plan seemed more desirable by the minute. If gold could buy happiness, then it could cure sick folks, too, including Johnathon Rucker. *Why, there was nothing that glowing chunk of metal couldn't do!* It could even give Chief a sturdy new roof. Heck, it could build him a castle! Gold was the dream granter, the wish giver, the great healer. No wonder so many souls worshiped it until death.

Scarlett-Rain bit her lip as the cold wind tugged on her hair. *"Gold is the great deceiver,"* the breeze whispered, but she didn't hear. Somehow, tomorrow felt lucky, and the day after that seemed even more promising. Scarlett-Rain's eyes were no longer wide with innocent starlight. She was ill, though she knew it not. The fever was silent and deadly. The symptoms were easy to overlook.

Scarlett-Rain placed her soft hand against her forehead. She didn't feel sick. With a shrug, she went back inside the house, and for the first time in many years, she went to bed without praying to God.

CHAPTER TEN

The Noble Chief

In the days leading up to the Calliway Fair, Scarlett-Rain, Caliber and Echo braved Papa's wilderness in search of gold. *Chieftain's Drink* roared with agitation as the two female explorers disrupted its once steady flow. Several times, it threatened to drown them, but Scarlett-Rain issued a sharp command that vibrated through the cool, quivering water.

"I am yer princess," she declared with her wild head held high, "and this is my knight and chambermaid."

With a grand sweep, she motioned to Caliber and Echo. "You betta not drown any of us!"

Groaning and cursing, the river retreated with quiet whispers. Echo shook her head at Scarlett-Rain, then shoved her pan back into the river's muddiest sweet spot. She had quickly grown used to her friend's strange conversations with the forest. Perhaps she was crazy, but what did that matter? She'd rather have a weird comrade than a normal one, anyway.

Suddenly, an idea exploded inside the child, and she ran across the slithering waves with her dress hiked up to her hip.

"Ask *Chieftain's Drink* where the gold is!" she said with a fierce tug on Scarlett-Rain's hair.

"Yeowch!"

Caliber chuckled while watching from the riverbank. With his nose stuck in the air, he let out a haughty sniff to show his distaste for being called a "knight" instead of a "king."

Scarlett-Rain and Echo stared at each other's dripping faces for a long moment. Springfield's seafoam eyes were glowing, as always, yet her left one was almost unrecognizable. An ugly gray and purple mass surrounded that innocent, glass-like eyeball as if threatening to consume it. Scarlett-Rain had cringed when she first saw it, but she tried not to flinch this time. *Why would someone beat their own child?* Even the wise wilderness had no answer.

"The river don't know where the gold is," Scarlett-Rain said simply, and Echo huffed.

"Maybe it's lyin' then!"

With her tiny back arched, the white-haired girl threw her head back to the sky as her sopping pigtails stuck against her brown cheeks.

"Hey, dumb woodland, whar's the gold?" Echo bellowed, and Scarlett-Rain grabbed her arm.

"Never insult the land," she warned. "Its ears are sharper than the ones God gave ter you, and forests can hold a grudge for decades."

Echo crossed her arms and raised the blonde eyebrow above her good eye. "Well, *you* ask it whar the gold is then!"

Scarlett-Rain glanced behind her at Caliber on the riverbank. With a snort, he turned his bear-like head away (obviously still offended over his knighthood), and Scarlett-Rain rolled her eyes. When she spun back around, Echo was still staring at her with her grotesque eye.

"Well?"

A long sigh escaped Scarlett-Rain's lips. She knew Papa's land would not welcome such a ridiculous request, but Echo's pitiful stare pierced harder than a jagged arrowhead. That child didn't deserve such a worthless family, but maybe gold could solve all her problems. Gold was the great rescuer, the hidden hero, and as Scarlett-Rain stared at Echo's wound, she realized how much the girl needed this one dream to come true.

"Alrite," Scarlett-Rain agreed with a grunt, and Springfield grinned.

With her long lashes closed over her eyes, Scarlett-Rain called out to the wilderness:

"Oh, mighty trees
and rivers, old,
won't you show us
to the gold?
My heart is sad.
My faith is shaken.
Take us to the path
less taken."

Echo grunted at her friend's silly poetry. In silence, they waited as a cool wind blew curiously through the shedding treetops. Scarlett-Rain didn't expect to hear the woodland's voices with Echo standing so near. After all, Springfield was a trespasser, and there was nothing the land hated more than someone who stood upon its ground, uninvited.

Suddenly, the hills yawned, and the dry, butterscotch grass shivered. A tall woodpecker beat a loud song against the bark of a fallen log. Like a sensible grandmother, stretching tree limbs seemed to shake their fragile fingers at Scarlett-Rain, and a chipmunk bickered with an impenetrable acorn. Scarlett-Rain closed her ears as the screeching rivers sang their reply:

"Oh, silly girls
who seek the gold,
stay away from here,
as you've been told.
The dream of gold
is but a lie.
Find it,
and someone shall die."

Scarlett-Rain lifted her hands, about to say more, but Echo yanked on her dress sleeve while pointing at the woods' edge. Chief was standing, black and dirty, on the riverbank with his beaver hat cocked to the side. A revolver was strapped across his middle (for men rarely traversed the woods without a weapon), and his pickaxe was dangling from his back. The autumn shadows on his face could not hide his yellow-tinted grin. Without thinking, Scarlett-Rain splashed through the river waves and crawled up the muddy bank to her love.

Laughing, Chief knelt down to pull her up the rest of the way, and for a breathless moment, she thought he might try to kiss her. They'd been together every day since Papa brought him home for supper. Each morning, Scarlett-Rain, Caliber and Echo would travel to the hill overlooking the mines, and there, they would spy on Johnathon as he worked. Ever the gentleman, Chief had kept his promise, and during his lunch break, he would meet Scarlett-Rain atop the hill to share cornbread, pear preserves and turkey. A rush of warm jolts shot across Scarlett-Rain's skin when Chief, unexpectedly, hugged her against his dirty shirt.

"Ya ready fer tomorrow?" he asked, referring to the fair, and Scarlett-Rain nodded.

Just then, Echo began climbing up the bank, and Johnathon quickly swung her up with his strong arms, as if she were a feather or scrawny stick. It's true that Rucker craved to be alone with Dillon Manchester's daughter, but the blasted wolf and little Echo were like ever-present, talkative shadows in her midst.

Instantly, Chief's walnut eyes rested upon the giant bruise on Echo's pinched, leather face.

"What happened to yer eye?" he asked bluntly, and he reached out to grab her pointed chin.

She didn't answer, and he examined her injury in silence for several moments as he held her jaw.

Scarlett-Rain squirmed. No one was ever bold enough to discuss the abuse Echo Springfield endured. It was rude to pry into other folks' business. There was a quiet mindset everyone in the wilderness agreed upon. Ignore evil, and it would eventually go away completely. Chief, however, did not seem familiar with this easy way of handling things.

"Was this yer pa's doin' or yer three, dopey brothers?"

Echo twitched and said nothing. Scarlett-Rain bit her lip.

After a moment, Johnathon released the child's chin and sighed.

"Ya know, I work with yer daddy and brothers," he said with almost a hiss of fire in his voice. Somewhere close by, a tree branch snapped. "I wonder what they'd have ter say about that bruise..."

Echo's large eyes widened, and she glanced at Scarlett-Rain, pleading with her in silence. Unsure how to react, Scarlett-Rain looked away.

Chief continued. "This mess ain't happenin' no more, Echo," he said to the trembling girl.

Scarlett-Rain reached out to touch the soot on his arm. "Chief—"

"No, I mean it." His gaze whipped onto his love with strict authority. "Someone's gotta stand up ter those idiots."

"They're her family," Scarlett-Rain reminded him, but Johnathon just blew loud air from his nose.

"I don't care. It ain't rite."

Echo's ocean-blue eyes welled with tears, and suddenly, her shrill voice rang out like a baby songbird.

"I'm gonna find the cure!" she cried, and for the first time since Scarlett-Rain had known her, she saw helplessness engulf the fierce child.

"What?" said Chief.

"The cure!" Echo wept again. "When I find the gold, my family'll stop hittin' me!"

Scarlett-Rain watched as Johnathon's hickory eyes scanned the girls' soaked dresses and then the river behind them. Caliber, the reluctant knight, was watching the scene a few feet away, and he howled something unrecognizable to Rucker.

"Gold ain't gonna cure yer stupid family," Chief said slowly to Echo. He seemed to be thinking over something invisible. "Gold ain't gonna solve anythin'." The last part he muttered as if it caused him great pain to speak aloud. His warm eyes rested on Scarlett-Rain.

"Welp," he continued, "if y'all wanna play pretend explorers, I reckon I'll come out here ter play with ya when I can." He raised a blackened finger to Echo. "But we ain't doin' this ter find gold, ya hear? If I find out about y'all huntin' fer gold again..." He looked straight into Scarlett-Rain's hazel eyes. "I'll tell Mr. Dillon."

For a moment, Scarlett-Rain thought Echo might pounce on Chief to attack him. Her blue eyes were wild and squinted, but Johnathon overlooked her. He tipped his fur hat to Scarlett-Rain.

"I gotta git back ter the mines," he said gruffly, and there was no hint of a smile on his uneven face. "I'll come git ya first thang tomorrah mornin', Scarlett-Rain."

Without a usual song on his lips, he walked away in silence. Caliber licked his fuzzy paws as if pleased with the coal miner for the first time. Scarlett-Rain turned to Echo. With a loud sob and heave, the girl crumpled into a ball on the ground.

"Go away, dumb brains!" she yelled to Caliber and Scarlett-Rain. "Go away!"

Ignoring her small demands, Scarlett-Rain and her dog watched Echo cry for, what must have been, a child's small eternity. Taking on Springfield's pain, *Chieftain's Drink* wept for the girl with a trickling, melodious song.

CHAPTER ELEVEN

Bully Boys

The night before the fair, Scarlett-Rain woke with a violent tremor in her bed. Gasping, she sat up to face the familiar darkness of the cabin loft. Someone was pounding on the door downstairs, and the soft glow of the murmuring fireplace below gently caressed the rafters in the ceiling. Papa's deep voice whispered something unrecognizable, and Scarlett-Rain heard the thud of his rifle being removed from the mantle above the fireplace.

Immediately, she leaped from her bed and threw herself against the edge of the attic floor. After rubbing her heavy eyelids, she peered down at Mama and Papa who were dressed in their nightclothes. A stranger still bellowed and banged on the wooden door, and Caliber howled from his corner. Dillon aimed his gun toward the door and motioned for Pleasant to open it.

Cold air rushed through the entrance, causing the weakened fire to hiss, and a tall man wearing a black coat and matching top hat stepped inside.

Instantly, Scarlett-Rain recognized the man's rusted orange beard and young, white face. It was the preacher of the little church in the hills—the church the Manchesters attended every Sunday during the warm months.

Dillon lowered his gun and reached out with his warm bear paw to grab the preacher's shoulder. "What's the trouble, Preacher?"

Scarlett-Rain was somewhat familiar with the man of God's midnight visits. Whenever there was mischief in Calliway, or at the church, or with the troublesome "hill people" deep in the wilderness, the preacher would come calling for Papa's assistance. Scarlett-Rain never knew the man's name. She just called him "Preacher," and that was good enough. It seemed logical to call a man by what he was.

"There's been a fight at the saloon, Dillon," Preacher said breathlessly. His gray eyes, like dew before a spring rain, were wide with anxiety.

"Who was it?" Dillon asked as Pleasant grabbed his heavy coat from alongside the door.

"A young buck named Johnathon Rucker," Preacher replied. "Goes by *Chief*. Poor lad! He took on the Springfield brothers!"

Pleasant gasped, and Scarlett-Rain's insides twisted and pinched themselves together.

"Why would he do a fool thang like that?" Mama said as the fireplace hiccupped and choked with her words. "Is he alrite?"

Preacher gave her a short nod, but his silver eyes iced over. "He's alrite, Ma'am, but you know how the Springfields are. By the time the fight was over, the Springfields had the whole saloon in an uproar! They was sayin' the boy jumped 'em, tryin' ter kill 'em. Well, you know how them boys are..."

He looked at Papa who was already shuffling inside his coat.

"I'm worried about the lad, Dillon," Preacher continued. "Them brothers is so riled up. I'm scared they gonna kill him if they get the chance."

Scarlett-Rain stifled a shriek, and Pleasant covered her pale lips with her slender fingers.

"Chief's new around here," Papa said with emotions of steel, but Scarlett-Rain could see the rare sliver of concern hidden within his coffee eyes. It dripped, like sweat, between the hardened lines on his face. "He don't know any better."

After a kiss upon Pleasant's mouth, Dillon strode out the door after Preacher. A cold rush swept across the floor, then dissolved alongside the fire's hot whispers.

Mama looked up at her daughter whose ghostly cheeks were flowing with tears. In perfect motherly fashion, she scurried over to the ladder and climbed up to embrace her only child. Scarlett-Rain didn't know how long they sat there, huddled up, sobbing together, but Mama's love was as warm and comforting as a burgundy-rose blanket.

Pleasant wept *with* her daughter, but she also wept *for* her daughter. It was a bittersweet kind of a cry—the kind of weeping that feels painful but heals at the same time. Scarlett-Rain's childhood was slipping away, like the very last dandelion fleck on a lonely stem. With every second that passed, Johnathon Rucker's love tugged at the fleck with a constant, gentle breeze. Very soon now, childhood would be dead, and only memories would remain in the brightest mist of morning.

Smiling, Pleasant pulled away and held her daughter's chin. She stared into her eyes for a long time and beheld the emerald forest that was still there.

"You love him," she said simply. "My darling, you love that boy."

Scarlett-Rain bit her lip. "Yes, Mama."

Even though her childish voice quivered, her spirit didn't. Loving Chief was the same as breathing. A baby isn't taught how to breathe, and a heart isn't taught how to love. Scarlett-Rain loved Chief, because that is how God intended it. Some things, the best things, are always eternal.

Mama smiled, and as she smiled, a single dandelion fleck was pulled away from its perch. Scarlett-Rain smiled back at Pleasant. Mama's face wasn't broken or defeated, but strong.

"Well, come on, Baby Cake," Pleasant said as she stood to turn down her daughter's bed covers. "It's still several hours before that boy comes callin' in the mornin', and ya need yer beauty sleep."

"Oh, Mama! Do you think he'll be okay? Do ya think he's hurt bad?"

"Of course, he's okay," Pleasant said simply. "You heard the preacher. Johnathon is fine."

She looked at Scarlett-Rain. "You'd best tell him ter stay away from them Springfield boys, though." Her splendid face wrinkled in thought for a moment. "I wonder whatevva made him wanna pick a fight with them rowdy boys, anyway..."

Holding her breath, Scarlett-Rain climbed into bed. She waited as Mama gave her a quiet kiss on the head, and she listened as Pleasant slid away muttering something about "boys and fighting."

Scarlett-Rain forced her eyes closed. She couldn't think about Echo. Chief was right to defend her, but he was like David facing Goliath without the help of God. The Springfields were angry, and they feasted on vengeance the same way a lot of folks feasted upon apple pie. Johnathon knew their dark secret, and monsters had a cruel habit of hating to be discovered.

With a restless moan, Scarlett Rain quickly gave in to slumber. Her nightmares punched and battered her spotless face, and somewhere in the wilderness, there was a cave that held a sleeping dragon. His teeth were made of pure, shining gold.

CHAPTER TWELVE

The Calliway Fair

Scarlett-Rain wasn't sure why, but the Calliway Fair smelled yellow, like the color of rust and honey. Whether that was a logical association or not, she didn't care. She tilted her head back as her black bun bobbed atop her scalp and inhaled the very real aromas of barbeque, fried sugar and cigar smoke. Yellow-colored or not, the fair smelled of adventure and trouble—*the most exhilarating aromas*, thought Scarlett-Rain, and somehow, the mixture of burnt, golden fragrances simply reminded her of Johnathon Rucker.

She'd hardly spoken a word to him on their way to the fair. This was mostly because Pleasant had laced her corset extra tight that morning, hoping to "accentuate her figure." Scarlett-Rain was used to wearing it loose or not at all—especially when running through the woods with Caliber. The things women did in the name of beauty seemed plain silly to Scarlett-Rain, and she wished to be a child again—wild and carefree.

In silence, she had sat behind Chief on his saddle with her scrawny arms wrapped around his middle. It was difficult to breathe, thanks to Mama's lacing, and she'd hoped Johnathon wouldn't notice. Fortunately, Chief had sung the entire way, and his horse traversed at an easy speed. Scarlett-Rain had tried to focus on the gentle, melodious sound of Chief's voice. His singing was like that of the tall timbers in Papa's wilderness. Many nights Scarlett-Rain had lain awake listening to the trees' somber lullaby. She never imagined a man, other than Dillon of course, could mimic those deep, ancient tones, but Chief's notes were something of a rarity. The forest had cowered in childish jealousy as they rode through Papa's land, and Scarlett-Rain smiled. Any human who could evoke nature's black envy was not really human, at all, but perhaps a spirit or memory—an angel sent from Heaven, for a time.

After they'd made it to the fair, Scarlett-Rain and Johnathon walked along the crowded dirt roads of Calliway, taking in the sights. All she could think about was the *death-trap* corset stretched across her middle, but Chief still seemed oblivious to her struggle. It was a cold but comfortable morning, and the buttercream shawl Pleasant crocheted for her daughter provided little warmth against the nipping wind. Ever the gentleman, Chief gave Scarlett-Rain his leather coat. It was lightweight but provided better protection against the breeze than a delicate wrap filled with pretty holes. Plus, Johnathon's jacket smelled good, like coffee, leather and coal.

"You look good in that coat," Chief said with a funny grin patched with dried-up blood. Scarlett-Rain looked up at his darkened, colorful face and smiled. His eyes, like tree bark and soot, were nearly lost amidst the purple, swollen mounds growing out of his eyebrows and cheekbones. Black patches of hair burst forth from his busted chin and jawline, and even though he was grinning foolishly, Scarlett-Rain knew he was in pain.

One thing was for certain, the Springfield brothers did not play nicely.

"You shouldn't have done it," Scarlett-Rain said breathlessly in reference to his saloon brawl the night before. In the nearby distance, she spotted the mercantile which was draped in crimson and navy banners and gaudy ribbon.

"Somebody had ter do it," said Chief, not the least bit sorry, "and I'll do it again—for Echo's sake. No child should have to live like that."

The chattering crowd shoved past the two of them, and Chief stopped in his tracks. Scarlett-Rain reached for the corset strapped across her stomach and sneaked a less-than-comfortable inhale.

"What's the matter with you?" he asked, ignoring her concern over the fistfight. Instantly, he eyed her hand, so delicately placed above her belly button.

Clutching the fabric of her pastel-yellow dress, Scarlett-Rain shook her head and let out a long gasp of air. Chief's wounded eyebrows raised in troublesome amusement.

"Wait a minute," he said as laughter slid across his cut lip.

Instinctively, he looked around as strangers shuffled by. Scarlett-Rain was staring down at Chief's boots and breathing like a woman in labor. She thought she heard Johnathon let out a grunt of guilty laughter.

"Did yer Mama hitch yer corset too tight this mornin'?" he chuckled and whispered too loudly. *Why did he have to be so blunt?*

Ignoring his insincerity, Scarlett-Rain just nodded as her lungs expanded like trapped ice.

"Come on," said Chief, "let's loosen that ridiculous thang—"

"I'll nevva let you!" Scarlett-Rain hissed with fake, lady-like dignity, but Johnathon just laughed again.

"Alrite, alrite," he said while holding up his hands like a little boy in surrender. "Let's keep walkin' then."

Just as he started to take a step, Scarlett-Rain grabbed hold of his loose, woolen shirt. "Johnathon, help me!"

An old woman passing by wrinkled her nose at the bent figure of Scarlett-Rain hunched over in her beau's jacket. Chief was laughing louder than a crow now, and he scooped up his girl and cradled her in his arms.

"Come on," he said again, "let's go find a quiet spot inside the fair."

Up and down the main dirt road of Calliway, the fair exploded like a kaleidoscope of colors. Funny men in face paint raced atop fat pigs while tossing rainbow balls through the air. Salesmen with slick voices, like shoe polish, were shouting about new plows and Herculean horses. Young women with scarlet eyelashes and hair ribbons twirled across the dirt, like dancers from a music box. Friendly gunshots screamed upwards toward the clouds as jumping kids in brown sacks tripped over too-large feet. Strange girls with long, seaweed hair and shiny fishtails peeked curiously out of the saloon's main window. Outside of the blacksmith shop, a man was yelling, "fortunes! Get your fortunes here! Today's yer lucky day, folks!" The fair was a dizzying spectacle of oddities and rare sights. It was youthful and mesmerizing, ripe with both innocence and mischief.

At the end of the long stretch of town, there was a wide, golden pasture, and in the middle of the field sat a giant, peppermint-striped tent—*a circus!* Scarlett-Rain felt her stomach leap with excitement of the unknown, and Chief chuckled when she gripped his shirt tighter.

Before reaching the field, Johnathon carried Scarlett-Rain inside a little alleyway between the bakery and the mercantile. Saying nothing, he sat her on top of a wooden barrel, and she winced from the pain of the corset.

Immediately, she shimmied out of Rucker's coat and the top of her dress (though her bosom was still modestly covered by her undergarments), and Chief quickly began to loosen the lace on the back of the corset. He kept peeking down the alley to make sure no one was watching, and when he turned back around, a voice reverberated through the passage.

"Ack! What are you doin', dumb brains?"

Scarlett-Rain and Johnathon turned to see Echo standing with her arms crossed at the end of the chamber. The child's dazzling blue eyes widened when she spotted Scarlett-Rain's pale shoulders sticking out the top of her chemise and Chief's dark hands fumbling with strands of long, pink ribbon.

Rocker groaned. "Ugh, can't we ever be alone?" he mumbled to himself, and Scarlett-Rain snapped at Echo.

"Go away, Springfield!"

Echo stuck her tongue out. "I'm tellin' on y'all!"

"Whoa!" Chief said to Echo, and he held his hands in the air. The corset was re-laced and plenty loose.

Ahhh... Scarlett-Rain inhaled the roguish air and sucked in the sweaty breeze, like a baby taking her first breath of life. Johnathon and Echo were bickering, but Scarlett-Rain just ignored them. *She could breathe again! ...Blast corsets! ...And blast beauty, too!*

Smiling, she pulled the yellow dress back over her shoulders and cuddled back inside Rucker's coat. With an amused sigh, she rolled her eyes at her companions.

"We weren't doin' anything!" Johnathon was arguing, clearly fearful of Dillon's wrath, but Echo was holding her fingers inside her ears while chanting, "I'm gonna tell! I'm gonna tell! I'm gonna tell!"

"It's alrite," Scarlett-Rain said to Johnathon, and she gave him a pink grin. Chief's annoyance appeared to melt away at his girl's reassurance. They walked over to Echo who scrunched her brown face into the meanest grimace she could muster.

"Y'all are stupid," she said. Then her crystal eyes widened when she saw Rucker's mauled face.

"What the blazes happened ter you? Now yer even uglier!"

"Echo!" Scarlett-Rain gasped, but Chief just chuckled.

"Trust me. It was worth it," he said, and Echo crossed her eyeballs at him.

"Where are you goin'?" Scarlett-Rain called, for the child sprinted off faster than a baby fox.

Echo didn't answer, but Scarlett-Rain knew where she was headed. *Chieftain's Drink* called across the wilderness and town with a lonely, silver song that sent chills racing across Scarlett-Rain's delicate skin. She glanced up at Chief, hoping he wouldn't guess where the child was going, but he knew. Disapproval was written all over his face as if someone carved it there with a stone and hammer. His black iron eyes rested on three large boys standing in the crowd. Their hair, like wheat, glinted yellow in the September sun, and they watched their sister as she ran away.

Quickly, their bullet eyes landed on Chief, and Scarlett-Rain saw hideous laughter and murder in their steady gazes. *Were they triplets?* She'd always wondered but didn't know for sure. They were tan and wore patched overalls. Like most miners, they seemed to appreciate the cool weather.

A few feet away from them stood their father, Willy, who looked exactly like them, only older, and his belly stuck out much further. He didn't see Johnathon or Scarlett-Rain, for he was busy chatting with his wife, Patty Springfield—*a miserable, blonde crow,* thought Scarlett-Rain.

"Come on," Chief said as he pulled Scarlett-Rain in the direction of the field and circus tent. "I'll be playin' my guitar inside The Big Top."

Scarlett-Rain walked alongside him, and she could feel the Springfield boys' steel eyes burning through them from across the short distance. Chief didn't seem to mind, though he undoubtedly felt the burning, too. He whistled a tune resembling, "Oh, Shenandoah," and he laughed when a clown fell off a squealing donkey nearby.

Scarlett-Rain giggled softly with him. However, it was a half-hearted sound, for *Chieftain's Drink* screeched louder than a phantom banshee across the timberlands. Scarlett-Rain's heart thudded icily against her chest, and the Springfields' stares flamed like demons from isolated mountains.

The warm color of brown burst through Scarlett-Rain's brain as it always did when Chief played his guitar. The audience, stuffed beneath The Big Top's red shadows, was silent. *Could they see and feel the music's colors as Scarlett-Rain could?* Most likely not. Scarlett-Rain learned long ago that only a rare few people could see the invisible, and even fewer could hear silent songs. Johnathon's tune was not silent, of course, but songs, like people, possessed souls. Closing her eyes, Scarlett-Rain saw the caramel soul of Rucker's melody, and she smiled.

Chief watched her face as he sang. To him, his love's face was a small moon glowing in the darkness of the tent. He loved her. He'd known it all along. It was only a matter of time before he asked her to share in his forever. The thought made him chuckle in the middle of his tune, but the random laugh only strengthened the melody with flawed perfection. This song was for her, and only her.

No one saw the Springfield brothers enter The Big Top, and no one saw them snatch the rope and whip away from the ringmaster. A lion roared from within his cage, and all at once, three giant shadows raced to the middle of the dirt arena and threw themselves upon the guitar player. Women shrieked, and men flung themselves from their seats in a desperate attempt to save the musician.

Scarlett-Rain tried to stand, to leap into action, but a large, iron hand held her down. The grip was so tight on her shoulder that she squealed from the pain as little stars danced before her eyes. The cloudy scents of smoke, whiskey and sweat invaded her nostrils. As she attempted to turn, a devil's face covered in black soot and ash pushed itself against her fair cheek. The smell of his panting breath was too much to bear, and his prickly jaw scratched her skin. With his other hand, the stranger squeezed the girl's face so tight that she thought her teeth might break.

"You stay outta our business, girl!" the demon demanded, and before he threw her to the ground, Scarlett-Rain saw the ugly, grime-eaten face of Willy Springfield. His red eyes blazed heavy with the fire of intoxication, and Scarlett-Rain clawed helplessly at his steel arms.

The circus tent was a madhouse now, with men throwing punches and kicks in any direction that seemed best. No one appeared to remember or even care why the brawl started, but any excuse to fight was a good enough reason. So, men whirled their knuckles at each other as women cried and bit (when necessary, of course).

Chief was lost amidst the ruckus, and the ringmaster looked on in bewilderment at this addicting, jaw-dropping performance. Never, in all his years as a showman, had he witnessed such an adrenaline-pumped show! It both frightened and gratified him.

With a grunt, Willy threw Scarlett-Rain to the ground with the same force and intensity he used to chunk heavy rocks out of the coal mines. A quick squeal escaped her lips, then everything went black...

CHAPTER THIRTEEN

Gold Country

Early the next morning, Scarlett-Rain woke in the softness of her own bed. Her eyelashes fluttered open, and Pleasant cried out in a song of joy as she flung herself upon her daughter. Mama had been weeping, but her toothy smile seemed radiant against the tears staining her chestnut cheeks. Gray and yellow swirls swam across Scarlett-Rain's vision. For several minutes, she didn't move as her thoughts tried to weave themselves back together.

A man was speaking a few feet away, and his quilted bag brushed against the end table. The misty swirls slowly formed a solid picture, and Scarlett-Rain clearly saw Mama's golden hair and the sleek, black hat of the doctor sitting next to the bed.

"See?" the doc said with a tired, yet cheerful, grumble. "I told ya she'd be alrite. No more worrying, Mrs. Manchester."

Pleasant lifted her head to stare into her daughter's eyes.

"Thank God yer awake!" she breathed as she embraced her again. "Ya had a mighty big blow ta yer head. What happened, Darlin'?"

Suddenly, the fog in Scarlett-Rain's vision slowly began to disappear, and the events of the fair came swarming back into her mind like cold ravens.

"Mama...where's Chief?"

The doc grumbled as Pleasant began stroking her daughter's forehead. "Shhhh...baby girl, he's alrite. Him and yer Papa waited here by yer bed all night. The doctor made 'em both go on ter work this mornin', so they wouldn't worry. He said ya were gonna be just fine!" Immediately, she glanced over her shoulder at the doctor and smiled.

"The lad's fine," Doc said in agreement with Pleasant. "I inspected him myself yesterday afta the fight." He looked at Scarlett-Rain. "You'd best remind the boy not ta go stirrin' up trouble with the Springfields. Leave them alone, and they'll leave you alone. Understand what I'm sayin'?"

"Mama?" Scarlett-Rain said again as something like fear bubbled up in her stomach.

Pleasant's youthful, porcelain face cracked for a moment. "What is it, Honey?"

Licking her lips, Scarlett-Rain struggled to find words to describe her encounter with Willy Springfield. She winced as black fear wrapped itself around her lungs as if to choke her.

"The fight wasn't Chief's fault!" she said defensively as she slowly sat up in her bed. She reached up and brushed her fingers against her cheeks in remembrance of Daddy Springfield's drunken grasp. "'Twas them Springfields' doin'! All four of 'em—the brothers and their paw—they came inta the circus tent and jumped Chief fer no reason!"

She stroked her jaw with a slight tremble in her fingers. "Mama? Willy Springfield pushed me..."

Pleasant's emerald eyes erupted like a green volcano. "Pushed you? What do you mean?"

With a troubled scowl, the doc leaned forward to hear what she had to say.

"I mean, he pushed me, Mama. During the fight, he walked behind me and grabbed me. He'd been drinkin' his potions, Mama. You know he's a wizard."

A silent gasp escaped Pleasant's lips, and she exchanged glances with the doctor who hid his rage behind a mask of stone.

After a moment, the doc reached out and patted Scarlett-Rain's shoulder.

"Don't you worry now, Miss. I'll mention this ta the sheriff. He's got them brothers down at the jail until they sober up. Sounds like their Daddy needs ta join 'em there." He sighed. "Best not mention this ta the lad, Chief. I don't want him gettin' inta any more fistfights. Let the law handle this one. Ya know what I mean?"

He glanced at Mama, and the volcano was suddenly quiet behind her eyes.

With a tip of his hat, he pulled his quilted bag off the table and stood. Pleasant thanked him with a jar of pear preserves, and he made his way down the ladder to leave.

"You rest fer a while, alrite girl?" he said to Scarlett-Rain as he climbed down.

Mama followed him down the steps and to the front door. When she returned to Scarlett-Rain's bed several minutes later, her regal face was pinched in silence as hot anger and worry fueled her racing thoughts.

"Yer little friend's waitin' fer you outside the front door," Pleasant said, her face emotionless.

"Echo?" asked Scarlett-Rain confusedly. Mama nodded.

Immediately, Scarlett-Rain pulled herself out of bed and began searching the room for her dress and boots. Pleasant sighed as she watched her.

"I shouldn't let ya go," she said, "but I reckon I can't stop ya. You'll end up sneakin' out if I say no." She let out a small groan. "No horseplay. Do ya hear me?"

Scarlett-Rain nodded. After a moment, she pulled the bright yellow dress over her head and pushed her boots on. Mama wrapped a warm shawl around her skinny shoulders, then helped her climb down the ladder. Caliber greeted them with disgusting kisses at the bottom. Quickly, Pleasant gathered some bread and preserves and placed them in a small potato sack.

"For lunch," she said as she handed it to her daughter. "Thar's enough fer yer little friend, and fer Johnathon, too."

Scarlett-Rain raised her eyebrow. *How long had Mama known she'd been meeting Chief each day for lunch at the cliff overlooking the mines?* Sometimes, Mama's wisdom was scary.

After a kiss from Pleasant, Scarlett-Rain bolted for the door.

"Ack!" Pleasant warned in a stern voice. "No runnin'! You betta take it easy!"

"Sorry, Mama."

Scarlett-Rain slowed her pace and exited the door with Caliber at her heels. Echo was standing there waiting with her arms crossed around her chest.

"My daddy's dumb," she said. "So are my brothers."

An ice-like sensation crawled across Scarlett-Rain's skin. Perhaps it was from the chill of the autumn wind, or perhaps it wasn't. Not sure how to respond, she just nodded in agreement.

Echo glanced at the closed door as if to make sure Pleasant wasn't listening. Scarlett-Rain wrinkled her face at the child.

"Where did you run off to yesterday?" she asked, already knowing the answer.

Springfield pulled her bony finger up to her lips. "Shhhhhhh!" She peeked at the door again, then back to her friend.

"I found the *gold!*" she said with fever in her wicked eyes.

Caliber growled for some unknown reason, and Scarlett-Rain pursed her lips in disgust over the child's lie.

"Shut up, Echo!"

With a grunt, Springfield started to whisper again. "Yer rich, Scarlett-Rain! Yer daddy's had the gold right here on his land this whole time!" The girl jumped slightly in her impish excitement. "Now you can marry that ugly ol' coal miner! We can cure Chief!"

Something inside Scarlett-Rain's stomach twisted at the mention of Johnathon's fever. Was it joy over Echo's words? Relief perhaps? Hope? *Nonsense,* Echo's boisterous tales were nothing but *nonsense*, and Scarlett-Rain shook her head.

"Chief's not sick," she said with her head held high, but part of her heart didn't trust her own declaration.

"Of course, he is," Echo said with a blunt tone.

Scarlett-Rain crossed her arms, and Caliber snorted. "I'm goin' ter wait fer Chief by the mines," she said, ignoring Echo.

"Don't ya wanna come see yer gold?"

Somewhere across the fields, the wilderness whispered a sharp warning. "*Go to the mines,*" it begged in a rust-covered song. "*Forget the gold.*"

Echo's sky-blue eyes were glowing with the intensity of summer, and Scarlett-Rain spotted something dreadful within the child's fanciful gaze...*truth*.

Before she knew it, Scarlett-Rain had forgotten Mama's command to "not run," and the three of them were sprinting off into Papa's wilderness. This time, it wasn't the woodland's familiar, silver voice that called but a sound much deeper and more solid. It was the rich, alluring promise of *gold*.

The trees were noisier than usual, whispering, frightened...sorrowful. Scarlett-Rain had never heard this new song of gold before, and she liked it. The melody was loud and powerful, like drums banging a determined call to war. For some reason, the Tennessee timbers cracked at that deafening, roaring sound. Gold's song drowned all reason and logic. It was a frightening masterpiece, in its own way, a symphony composed by sinful ghosts of history. Scarlett-Rain knew where the gold was. It had

been near to her all along, just waiting to be discovered...
to be remembered.

Chieftain's Drink twinkled bright gray and white in
the close distance, but that's not where the trio was
headed—not quite. Gold's song was leading them to a
place much darker than the river...somewhere vaguely
familiar.

Not far from *Chieftain's Drink*, there was a cave on
Papa's land. The mouth was hidden amongst thick brush
and brambles as if the woodland itself tried to devour it
long ago. The entrance was boarded up by Dillon many
years before his only child was born, but Scarlett-Rain
remembered seeing the cave, once, when she was almost
the height of Papa's knees.

In her steel heart, she knew that same cavern was
where Echo was leading them. Her bones ached with the
gnawing truth of their destination. *What secret was the
dragon made of rock hiding?* Even more mysterious was
the question, *why did Papa hide it away so long ago?*

The cave's beastly head rose out of the ground like a
stone serpent wearing a crown of faded emerald green
and crimson. Its teeth were rotted wooden planks jutting
out in grotesque directions. There was a black hole in its
wicked smile as if an iron fist had punched through his
grin.

Scarlett-Rain and Caliber stopped. The wildwood held its breath. Boards and nails were scattered across the ground by Echo who had explored inside the heart of the beast just yesterday. Caliber growled, and his master gasped in perfect pitch.

At that moment, the trees' green canopy cracked, and a thin sliver of sunlight lit upon the black opening of the cave. Caliber howled with the pain of a hundred wild wolves fastened down with metal chains, and Scarlett-Rain let loose a silent wail, like an enchanted witch casting some foreign curse or spell.

Yellow gold, resembling space dust, glittered and glowed, like a million eternities, from within the throat of the dragon. The symphony of wealth exploded and roared with a deafening finale. *What a show! What a dangerous, enrapturing spectacle!* The explorers' dream had come true. They had found gold, *the great deceiver, the wish granter, the dream giver...*

"I..." Words failed Scarlett-Rain for a long time. The three of them stood there, staring deep within the mouth, panting and gasping for air. Their hearts beat louder than gold's own drums.

"I...don't believe it..." Scarlett-Rain finally managed to spit out.

Caliber made a hacking noise as if the girls disgusted him more than the gold did.

Suddenly, the rush of realization plummeted, from the sky perhaps, and pounded Scarlett-Rain hard in the chest. "WE'RE RICH!"

Singing and chanting like spoiled devils, the girls began dancing with one another, jumping up and down in glorious elation. Caliber puffed, like a stinky sad-sack, and curled into a ball on the grass.

"I'll buy you a new dress!" Scarlett-Rain laughed wildly.

"I'll buy you a new house!" Echo added with lightning delight.

"We'll buy the whole dang town!"

Caliber rolled his eyes as the explorers shouted their victories.

"Wait a minute!" Scarlett-Rain said, her voice shaking in giddiness. "I gotta go tell Chief!"

"Heavens to Betsy!" Echo yelled. "Are you hopin' that hideous toad'll kiss ya or somethin'?"

Springfield roared with laughter again, and before she knew it, Scarlett-Rain had jumped on her to throw playful punches. The two of them rolled into the cave as golden light, like stardust and heaven flakes, splattered across their glowing skin. Suddenly, they stopped their roughhousing and stared at the wonder all around them.

The scene was breathless, heartless, perhaps frozen in time. It was beautiful.

"Why do ya suppose yer papa hid it away?" Echo asked, still staring transfixed at the tunnel wrapped in gold.

It took Scarlett-Rain a moment to respond. She'd forgotten about Papa, and her heart skipped a beat. Suddenly, she felt as if she'd dug up a dark burden from his past, a painful secret that was meant to be buried away forever.

She shook her head. It didn't make sense. *Why would any man hide away his worldly wealth? Why would Papa throw away his treasure like useless rock?* For a guilty minute, she felt angry at him.

Fever running hot in her veins, Scarlett-Rain pushed the thought of Dillon from her mind.

"Come on," she said to Echo, not even noticing her own trembling hands. "Let's go tell Chief!"

CHAPTER FOURTEEN

Fever Maiden

Scarlett-Rain's body did not stop shaking all the way to the cliff overlooking the mines. She spotted Chief's lean figure, brown and dusty in the morning sun, almost instantly as she peered over the edge. Despite the chilly air, warm goosebumps pranced across her tingling skin.

Echo scowled at her friend's love-struck face.

"I'll nevva understand what you see in him," she said as she spat like a man.

Scarlett-Rain cocked her head to the side and stared at Springfield. "You should be nicer ta him, especially after all he's done fer you."

Echo made a mean, wretched face at her companion's words. "What do ya mean?"

"I mean, Chief stands up fer you, Dummy," Scarlett-Rain said. "He defends ya against yer crazy, good-fer-nothin' family. Why do ya think he got beat-up, Silly?"

Echo went silent for a long while as her eyes searched the mines below. Finally, she softly said, "he didn't have ter do that fer me. I don't need help. The gold'll fix everythin'."

Scarlett-Rain raised her eyebrows, about to speak again to Echo, but down below the cliff, Chief stopped his work to give the spies a cheerful wave. With a lopsided grin, he blew a kiss to Scarlett-Rain, and she found herself imagining what the taste of that kiss might be like if it were planted on her lips. *When was he going to kiss her—for real?* She wondered. Then, with a bit of fear and curiosity, she began twisting her lips in funny movements trying to practice for the main event. Echo snorted as she watched Scarlett-Rain.

The minutes passed in silence, and the girls watched Chief work. Caliber yawned and lay down beside his master. Out of the blue, Echo asked, "did my paw hit you yesterday?"

Scarlett-Rain nearly choked on her own spit.

"Yes," she replied after a steady pause.

"Oh."

Neither of them said a word, and Caliber's stomach made a random gurgling noise.

"My paw's always like that...when he drinks his potions," Echo added. "My brothers are just like 'im." She sighed as if the confession caused her great pain. "It's all okay, though. The gold will fix everythin'."

Scarlett-Rain reached out to touch Springfield's shoulder. "Echo, you can't tell yer family about the gold. You gotta keep it a secret."

"Why?" Echo almost hissed. A faint fire glimmered in her blue eyes, and her pink lips formed a narrow line. "Why can't I cure my family, but you get ta cure yer dream man?" Her gaze darted down to Chief in the same way a whip might slap a horse. "Not fair!"

Scarlett-Rain said nothing, and she stared back down at Johnathon.

When the sun was higher in the sky, Chief set aside his pickaxe and ran to the top of the cliff. Sweat poured down his shirt, despite the chill in the air, and he wiped the coal from his bruised face. Scarlett-Rain, Echo and

Caliber turned when he appeared behind them. A light song filled his lungs, and he gave his love a crooked smile from beneath his beaver hat.

Scarlett-Rain smiled in return, hoping Echo wouldn't mention the "kissy" faces she had been making earlier, and Johnathon hurried to sit alongside her.

"I'm so glad you're feelin' better!" he said happily to his love, but Echo cut him off.

"Don't even bother sittin' down!" Springfield proclaimed as she jumped up toward the sky. "We got somethin' ter show ya, dumb brain!"

Chief looked at Scarlett-Rain. What's she talkin' about?"

"Come on!" Scarlett-Rain said excitedly as she pulled him by his wet arm.

Again, the explorers bounded through the forest, past *Chieftain's Drink*, and on toward *The Dragon's Head* (the name newly bestowed upon the gold mine). Scarlett-Rain's body trembled again as they neared the cave, and Johnathon noticed her quivering.

"What's this all about?" he asked eagerly and with a bit of suspicion.

"Hold yer horses!" Echo called out in singsong.

When they reached the cavern, the drumbeat of gold rang softer this time, but still with fervor. Chief stared at

The Dragon's Head and the trail of nails and boards that were thrown across the grass. He was clueless as to what was going on, and the song of wealth was silent against his ears.

Echo motioned for him to walk inside the wide, black mouth, but Johnathon hesitated in consideration. Finally, after seeing Scarlett-Rain's sun-lit face, he took her hand, and all of them walked inside (except for Caliber, the knight, who stood stubbornly outside).

When Chief's brown eyes gazed upon the gold for the first time, his face revealed his wonder and bewilderment. Every muscle in his jaw and cheekbones seemed to twist in brand-new, unthinkable positions, and Scarlett-Rain wasn't sure if his face would ever regain its natural form. For a long time, he was breathless and silent beneath nature's miracle. What he was thinking, no one could tell, but one thing was for certain. Johnathon, the man who could hear silent songs, like Scarlett-Rain, heard no music there in the depths of that mine. For him, the beast's great belly was quiet, and he looked at Scarlett-Rain and Echo with fear in his eyes.

"Y'all disobeyed me," he accused, and Scarlett-Rain felt the burning sting of his words. Suddenly, he grabbed her by the arm the way a hero might grab someone who was in danger. His voice was low and desperate. Scarlett-

Rain had never seen him so rattled. His reaction to the gold—his cure—was all wrong, and to Scarlett-Rain's shock, she felt angry at him.

"Come here," he said to Echo, his voice resembling Dillon's at that moment.

Startled, Springfield walked over and stood beside Scarlett-Rain. On the inside, Rucker was fuming, but his composure was as still and focused as *Chieftain's Drink* on a windless afternoon.

"Y'all disobeyed me," he said again as his grip tightened on Scarlett-Rain's arm. *Was he panting?*

"Listen to me," he continued. "This stays between us." His eyes appeared black beneath the shadow of the gold. "Do you understand?" The last part, he almost yelled.

The girls nodded, completely taken aback by his reaction. He cursed, not bothering to apologize, and stared up at the gold the way one might look upon a demon or threatening beast.

"This stays between us," he mumbled again, and his eyes shot back to the girls. "Swear it. Swear that you won't breathe a word about the gold to anyone."

Johnathon was pacing back and forth now, muttering to himself. "Mr. Dillon had this mine hidden away for a reason...he didn't want it—any of it...can't say I blame him..."

Tears filled Echo's eyes. "But this is yer cure, dumb brain!" she shouted at Chief. "You got the fever! It's the only way you'll git ter marry Scarlett-Rain!"

Johnathon stopped in his tracks and looked at her. "You think *I* got the fever?" He eyed the two of them standing before him as if hoping they would examine their own hearts. Then he chuckled. "Thar's only two people down inside this darn cave who have gold fever..." His eyes twinkled with truth. "...and it ain't me."

Scarlett-Rain bit her lip, and Echo burst into tears. Suddenly, Springfield ran out of the mine, muttering childish insults as she went.

Scarlett-Rain reached for her friend, as if to hold her captive, but Chief said, "let her go."

Caliber barked at Springfield as she ran into the forest, and Scarlett-Rain was left standing alone inside *The Dragon's Head* with Chief.

"I'm sorry," she said to him as teardrops filled her lids. *How long had she been sick with the fever?* She didn't know. "I'm so sorry."

"It's alrite," Johnathon said almost instantly, and there was forgiveness etched all over his face of soft stone.

"W-what i-is the c-cure?" Scarlett-Rain muttered, foolishness taking root in her bones. "W-what h-heals gold fever?"

Suddenly, Chief pulled her against his sticky shirt. The light dancing off the gold glittered across his arms. His calm face and fur hat reflected a kaleidoscope of yellow and orange illumination.

Heat seized Scarlett-Rain as Johnathon placed his lips against her forehead. His skin was warm, like a comforting fireplace, against the cold air inside the cave.

"Love..." he whispered against her brow. "Love heals the fever..."

"Is that what healed you?"

Gently, his lips kissed her closed eyes and then her cheek. A tidal wave rushed over Scarlett-Rain like burning flames strengthening her spirit. She was powerless against its severity, and she wished it would never end. Her greatest desire was that this new, passionate blaze would consume her forever.

"Yes," Chief breathed against her lips, "love heals us all."

With that statement, he wrapped his arms so tight around the fever maiden and kissed her hard. Not even all the water in *Chieftain's Drink* could quench that fire.

CHAPTER FIFTEEN

The Dragon's Head

Papa's gold was not the only secret Scarlett-Rain kept hidden over the next few weeks. She didn't dare tell *anyone* about the way Chief had kissed her that day deep inside the cave. Whether he meant for it to or not, Johnathon's kiss lingered, and Scarlett-Rain discovered there were "side effects" of being kissed by one's true love for the very first time. No matter what she did, she could not stop smiling and singing as the days passed by, and several times, Papa mentioned her "high spirits." Being naïve, as fathers sometimes are, Dillon concluded that the autumn weather was the reason for his daughter's cheerful mood, and Scarlett-Rain let him live in ignorant bliss.

Mama, however, being a bit more fluent in the romantic arts than her husband, watched their daughter with an attentive, knowing eye.

"I think I hear weddin' bells..." she hinted too often in front of Dillon, hoping he might understand her worries about two unmarried kids deep in love. "...But not until she's sixteen—*sixteen*."

Most of the time, Papa would just grunt, not understanding his wife's cues, or perhaps choosing not to. Either way, the day finally arrived, just a few short weeks after Scarlett-Rain and Chief's first kiss, when Johnathon Rucker came knocking on Dillon Manchester's door. He desired more than just a secret kiss with Scarlett-Rain beneath *The Dragon's Head*. He wanted to spend the rest of his life with her.

"Mr. Dillon," Chief said one night at the Manchesters' supper table. He cleared his throat, and Scarlett-Rain noticed his hand shaking against his mug of hot coffee.

"Yes?" Papa said through a mouthful of mashed potatoes.

Pleasant held her breath, sensing what was coming, and Scarlett-Rain could feel Chief's rare anxiety burning through the wooden table.

"Mr. Dillon," Chief began again, "I love yer daughter. I'd die fer yer daughter. I...I wish ta marry her."

Papa continued eating his taters, and Scarlett-Rain thought she saw him glance up at his rifle above the mantle.

The silence was intense, and even Caliber grew nervous for Chief within the shadows of his smelly corner.

After what seemed like a decade, Papa folded his large hands together and faced the man who would soon take his place.

"I love my daughter," Dillon said in the most serious tone Scarlett-Rain had ever heard. "As her father, my prayer has always been fer the Lord ta give her a husband who will love her more than I do."

Rucker nodded.

"Do you love my daughter more than I do, boy?" Dillon asked.

Unsure how to answer such a question, Chief nodded again. "Sir, I love her with all my heart...all my soul...all I have ta give."

Was Mama crying? Scarlett-Rain refused to look at her.

Without a smile, Papa gave his answer—the most painful words he would utter for as long as he lived.

"Johnathon Rucker, I give you my daughter."

Scarlett-Rain let out a loud gasp, and Chief gave her a relieved wink and grin. Mama's silver sobs of joy filled the warm cabin, and Caliber bounded over to lick his new master's face.

"But not until she's sixteen!" Mama added.

Suddenly, the room erupted in laughter, and Pleasant yelled, "give her a kiss, Johnathon!"

Chief flushed (which was indeed rare for him) and reached across the table to plant an awkward peck on Scarlett-Rain's mouth. Kissing in the depths of a dragon's ferocious head was one thing, but kissing in front of parents was something else entirely. Scarlett-Rain's cheeks turned as red as her name.

Just as Papa went to grab his banjo, a gunshot rang out across the wilderness.

"Now, who could that be?" Pleasant wondered aloud. "Someone's shooting on our land."

Papa's musical face turned into a grimace. Scarlett-Rain and Chief looked at each other.

The land screamed out in a haunting song of fear. Black and silver notes rolled into a sharp, spine-tingling melody. Scarlett-Rain covered her ears, for the tune was agonizing, like a knife slicing through clean skin. Never before had the wildwood called out for help with such a ghostly screech. Even Mama and Papa appeared to hear its plea.

"Somethin's wrong," Dillon said, reading their thoughts.

Without a word, he grabbed his rifle and looked at Mama and Scarlett-Rain.

"Stay here, girls," he said, but before he could finish speaking, his daughter bolted out the front door, leaving it swinging in her midst.

Papa and Chief raced after her across the field, and Johnathon caught up to her first.

"Go back home, Scarlett-Rain," he urged as he ran alongside her. "It could be dangerous."

"No," she replied in defiance. "You know it's about the gold! I won't let you or Papa git hurt!"

Chief cursed again with no apology, and Scarlett-Rain sprinted until her legs felt like they might collapse. Johnathon kept up with her with ease. Papa remained in the distant rear.

The forest's call was louder now, and Caliber, the reluctant knight, appeared like a phantom out of the shadows. Scarlett-Rain could feel her heart ripping inside her chest with every somber chord the wilderness struck. *Whose gun had fired on Papa's land?* The answer was obvious, and the wildwood shrieked it loud and clear... *Springfields!*

The Tennessee timbers resembled tall, brown ghosts, and the black hills and baby mountains looked like parasites sucking life from the land. *Chieftain's Drink* sparkled in the close distance. They were almost to the cave now...any minute and...

Another gunshot pierced through the cold night air, and a star blinked from high above as if wounded by the sound of the stray bullet.

"Springfields!" Chief shouted with rage, mimicking the cry of the land. His revolver was aimed right at the intruders.

There they stood, four giant, husky men, staring straight into the mouth of the dragon. Their blond heads appeared ethereal in the moonlight. One of them was clutching his belly, wounded from the blast no doubt, and he cursed when he spotted Chief and Scarlett-Rain.

"Paw, ya shot me!"

Were they fighting? Scarlett-Rain could hardly believe it. They were brawling over Papa's gold, and blood was spewing from Henry Springfield's middle. The two uninjured brothers immediately raised their pistols in Chief's direction. Scarlett-Rain could smell their whiskey from several yards away, and to her horror, she saw Echo's pearl-white head, like star-silk, peeking out of the mouth of the cavern. *The secret was out.*

"Echo!"

The female Springfield reached for Scarlett-Rain the way a baby might stretch out her hand for her mama, but the four giants were blocking the way. Scarlett-Rain couldn't go to her friend's aid.

Suddenly, Dillon's grizzly bear voice roared through the night. "What's the meanin' of this, Willy?"

Chief and Scarlett-Rain watched as Papa stepped out of the trees. His rifle was aimed for the leader of the clan, and when Mr. Springfield saw his co-worker and closest neighbor, he let out a manic, drunken laugh.

"Are you gonna shoot me, Dillon?" He growled and stumbled. Willy's gun was lying on the ground next to his feet. One of his uninjured sons pointed his firearm straight at Mr. Manchester, and the other boy kept his targeting Chief.

Scarlett-Rain had never seen her papa so still. Even though he must have been frightened, his body was firm and in control.

"You've done shot yer boy in yer drunken raid," Papa said simply, and Willy laughed, clearly out of his mind at that moment.

"You liar," said the Goliath man as he wiped spit from his mouth and tripped over his boots. "I'm the best shot in Tennessee, and I'd nevva shoot my own kin—my own blood. Yer a fool, Dillon."

"Paw!" Henry cried out with another curse.

Slowly, Chief inched closer to where Mr. Manchester was standing, while keeping Scarlett-Rain hidden behind his own body for protection. Scarlett-Rain could see Johnathon's black revolver glinting in the skylight. It was aimed toward one of the brothers. When the young man saw Chief move, his own raised weapon followed the musician's chest.

"How long you been hidin' the gold away?" Willy slurred his words as he moved toward Dillon's gun.

"Yer boy needs help, Willy," Dillon said almost softly.

"NO, HE DON'T!" Mr. Springfield spat at Papa's boots. "He's fine, you blasted IDIOT!"

Henry was moaning on his knees now with his fingers clutching his stomach. Echo was cowering in the dragon's mouth with her hands cupped over her ears.

"Willy, don't be a fool," Dillon tried to reason again. "Y'all are drunk, and yer boy's dyin'—"

"Put down yer guns and let us help him!" Chief croaked to the intoxicated brothers.

Suddenly, Henry fell face-first into the dirt. Johnathon started to jump to his aid, but Dillon held him back with one hand.

"Leave him be!" Willy bellowed. "Can't m'boy just take a nap? Is that a crime?"

"Stealin' another man's property is a crime," Dillon said, "and if yer boy dies, you'll be charged with murder."

Henry's enormous body gave a single twitch on the ground, then froze. Echo screamed. The Springfield men didn't move.

"Let us have the gold, Dillon," Willy said, appearing somewhat sober for a moment. "Give us the gold, and we'll let you live."

Papa's eyes rested on a tiny, horrified ghost peeping out of the gold mine, and he knew what he must do. He cleared his throat.

"Give us yer daughter, Springfield," Papa replied. "Give us yer daughter, and you can have the gold."

Instantly, whatever sanity remained on Willy's bushy face vanished, and he screamed in madness.

"Nevva! I'll nevva give up my daughter! Give me the gold!" Mr. Springfield's wild eyes spotted Scarlett-Rain standing behind Chief. "I told you ter stay outta our business, girl!"

Out of nowhere, Willy pulled out a knife and made a savage dive for Scarlett-Rain. Johnathon's revolver rang out first and punctured a black hole in the middle of Willy Springfield's chest. His massive body hit the ground as he hollered and kicked at the air.

Like a wisp of smoke, Echo darted for her pa. The two brothers, not noticing their sister, fired at Chief. One bullet grazed Johnathon's shoulder, and he let out a moan. The other bullet skimmed right past Echo, barely missing her neck. She screamed and fell to the ground with her hands cupped over her ears.

Suddenly, a shadow stepped out of the woods. Pleasant's sweet face was as rigid as a statue. In her steady arms was one of Papa's guns she'd brought from home. She pointed it straight at the two brothers.

"Put yer weapons down, now," she commanded.

The brothers looked at each other. With both Papa and Mama aiming their rifles at them, they had no choice but to surrender. Shaking their heads, they threw down their guns, and Dillon rushed to pick them up.

Pleasant instinctively ran for little Echo (who was crying) and hugged her in her arms. "It's alrite. It's all over now," she whispered as she rubbed the child's back.

Chief was wincing as he clutched his shoulder. Scarlett-Rain tore off a piece of her petticoat to tie around his bleeding wound.

"Don't worry about me," he said with a pained grin. "It's just a scratch."

Papa hurried over to Henry and Willy's bodies to check for any signs of life. With a heavy sigh, he looked up and shook his head. The two brothers were too intoxicated to understand, but Echo knew. Her sobs sailed even louder across the air.

Caliber, who had been hiding in the shadows, emerged and ran for the child. He began licking her skinny arms as Pleasant sang a lullaby. Chief and Scarlett-Rain were holding hands with their heads bowed low in sorrow for their friend.

Dillon pointed his rifle at the two brothers. "I reckon y'all know where we're goin'," he said. "It seems the sheriff let y'all outta jail too early after the circus incident. Y'all will have a lotta time ter think about what happened here tonight." He glanced at the motionless figures of Willy and Henry.

"Papa?" said Scarlett-Rain. "Can Echo stay at our house tonight?"

Dillon gave a solemn smile. "I wouldn't have it any other way." He looked at Johnathon. "Come on, boy. Help me escort these brothers to their cage. While we're in town, the doc can take a look at yer shoulder." He glanced back at the bodies of Henry and Willy. "We'll hafta come back with the sheriff and bury 'em."

In silence, Papa and Chief led the Springfield boys into the darkness.

Scarlett-Rain ran to Echo and Mama, and the three of them embraced each other.

"I'm sorry," Echo hiccupped through her tears. "The cure didn't work..."

Scarlett-Rain grabbed her hand. "We was wrong, Echo. Gold ain't the cure for sickness. *Love* is."

"Love?" said the child. "What's love?"

Pleasant hugged the girl tightly. "Well, you've got a whole life ahead of ya that's gonna be filled with it."

CHAPTER SIXTEEN

Renewed

Two days later, the sheriff came to visit the Manchesters' cabin. Papa, Mama and Chief were sitting at the dining table with the lawman while Scarlett-Rain and Echo looked down from the loft. With a sigh, the sheriff removed his wide hat and set it on the table before him. Caliber moaned from his corner.

"Well, the Springfield brothers are gone," said the man with the shining gold star on his vest.

"Gone?" repeated Mama with a look of horror. "What do ya mean, *gone*?"

The sheriff continued with a low grumble. "I mean, the good people of Calliway decided ter take matters inta their own hands... They ran the brothers out of town— ran their Ma out, too. I've nevva seen so many folks riled up."

Chief groaned. "They'll come back."

The sheriff cleared his throat. "That's what I've come ter talk ter ya about, Dillon." He looked at Papa. "Naturally, everybody knows about yer gold now... If the Springfields don't come back fer it, then somebody else will..."

Papa's eyes lifted to the ceiling as if in silent prayer. A rare tear fell down his cheek, which was hard and crumbling like coal.

"I hid it away..." he admitted to them, referring to the gold mine. "Years ago, I hid it away."

"Why, Papa?" Scarlett-Rain asked from the loft above. She remembered the loud drums of gold's melody that sang to her heart the first time she looked upon the glowing metal. *Did Papa ever hear that song?* Perhaps Dillon, like Chief, was one of the rare few men who stood in gold's presence and heard the beautiful, sacred sound of *nothing*.

"I hid it away to prevent all this," Papa answered, and his great chest heaved as he waved his hand around toward the sheriff and the invisible chaos that had erupted in recent days.

"I'm the richest man in the world," he continued after a moment, "not because of the gold, but because of you, my love..." He looked at Pleasant. "And you, my darlin'..." He looked at Scarlett-Rain. "I'm rich because of God's holy spirit that lives in me." He paused as his large hand came to rest over his heart, and his great face turned toward the window and the wilderness in the distance. "Death is wealth's only reward."

Everyone was silent for a long time and then Chief spoke. "Then let's git rid of it, Mr. Manchester," he said. "Let's git rid of the gold."

"How are we gonna git rid of a cave?" the sheriff asked, perplexed.

Dillon already knew the answer, and he nodded at Johnathon with a new sparkle (or perhaps flame) in his eyes.

Chief grinned at the sheriff, and he gave Scarlett-Rain a wink. "Oh, we coal miners have our ways..."

That very night, just before a crimson sunset faded through the fabric of a gray sky, *The Dragon's Head* breathed its last. All the land shook from the thunder of that final roar. The ancient rock and glowing yellow metal exploded in thunderous flames, and black clouds growled as smoke licked away the cursed treasure.

Johnathon, Echo and the sheriff were standing with the Manchesters a great distance away from the explosion (for protection). With wide eyes, they beheld that wonderous fire that burned away all their troubles at once.

Chief hollered and hooted loudly, like a wild boy enjoying something as simple as a fireworks display, and he shook Dillon's shoulder in joy. Pleasant gave her husband a kiss on the cheek as Scarlett-Rain and Echo danced with Caliber.

Dillon Manchester would be forever remembered as the man who destroyed his gold in exchange for a simple life of peace and contentment. Some would say he was foolish. Others would proclaim his wisdom, like Solomon of old. Either way, the gold was gone, and the Manchesters were grateful for it. They knew that real riches were born of the soul, not the world.

Scarlett-Rain smiled. Fresh memories soared into her cloudless mind the moment the gold blew away forever. She could hear those memories now, like lightning bugs twirling in rhythm to a silent tune. There was no better sound in the world than autumn laughter chiming in a calm breeze or a guitar dueling a banjo in playful harmony. There was no better melody than that of blue windchimes playing every time Papa kissed Mama. There was no greater joy than the brown voice of Chief whispering of love...*love.*

Those simple moments, little memories floating on the wings of fragile hummingbirds...those were life's greatest treasures.

When the earth stopped shaking and the gold was gone forever, the sheriff pulled little Echo off to the side.

"Are you happy?" he asked. "I mean...with the Manchesters? Will you be happy with them?"

To his relief, the child nodded. She pointed to the glowing smoke and flames that licked up the cave. "My past was in there," she stated.

With tears in his eyes, the lawman nodded, too. "That's right," he said.

All at once, Papa's wilderness began to sing. It was a song of praise, a song of rejoicing over what was to come, a song of *real* gold—the kind that flames could never destroy. The land's chorus erupted in a silver symphony as tiny stars danced across their gray stage. "*Renewed,*" hummed the rivers' and timbers' sweet voices, "*renewed.*"

Chief took Scarlett-Rain's hand. Never had such a beautiful song been witnessed by human ears.

The fever had run its course.

CHAPTER SEVENTEEN

Love Forevermore

On a morning in early spring, Johnathon and Scarlett-Rain were waiting to be wed. He was eighteen years old now, and she had been sixteen for one whole day. The air was cold and windy, and pumpkin brush strokes poured across gray clouds. The two lovers stood facing each other in front of the circus tent left behind by the Calliway Fair last September. The candy-cane-colored "Big Top" contrasted sharply against the soft, yellow field, which was wide with the birth of spring. Little martins chirped and sang happily in the air above. Caliber, the now *proud* knight, was standing beside his two masters.

Chief was gazing down at Scarlett-Rain and grinning as he held both her hands in his. She knew he was nervous about the small crowd gathered to hear their vows, but he didn't show it.

"You look beautiful," he said as he leaned down to whisper in her ear.

Scarlett-Rain smiled with pinkish delight. Her wild, charcoal hair fell loosely across her shoulders and back, and atop her head was a simple veil that Mama had worn when she married Papa. The dress, too, was Pleasant's wedding gown—ivory, cream and graceful, just like Mama.

Papa was sitting alongside his wife and Echo in the first row of chairs that had been placed in the field for the ceremony.

"Where's the preacher?" Scarlett-Rain heard him ask, and suddenly, the gatherers started chatting about the whereabouts of the tardy minister.

Chief whispered again to his love, "Can I sing ya a song while we wait?"

Scarlett-Rain blushed and nodded as he laid his head against hers. Suddenly, his quiet song filled her heart with familiar brown warmth.

"Are you going to the Calliway Fair,

where the cold is heavy on the wilderness?

Please, Fever Maiden, won't you meet me there?

For you have always been my heart's desire."

Chuckling, he kissed her forehead, then pulled away slightly to stare at her face, which was bright and dew-covered. She giggled with glee and caressed his prickly jaw with her fingers.

Just then, the crowd began to find their seats, for Preacher was trudging up the field toward the ceremony. His red head was glistening bronze in the morning light. "Better late than nevva," Papa grumbled, and Pleasant slapped him playfully on the shoulder. Echo snickered, then stuck her tongue out at the bride and groom.

Chief's crooked smile, so boyish and full of mischief, caused liquid joy to spill over Scarlett-Rain's heart. The loyal aromas of coal and leather wrapped around her, and surprisingly, she let loose a happy laugh.

Chief raised one thick eyebrow and gazed at her with his coffee-tinted eyes.

"Are you happy?" he asked.

Scarlett-Rain nodded as cozy dizziness swarmed around her head, like friendly bumblebees.

"Today is beautiful," she said suddenly. "Today is beautiful, because I love you, Johnathon Rucker. Let the land and all the world be witness to it, because love...love is everything."

For a long moment, Chief just stood grinning, and a cold breeze swept through his dark hair.

"Can I go ahead and kiss ya?" he asked eagerly. "Nobody's watchin', and the blasted preacher's walkin' slow on purpose."

Without bothering to wait for her reply, Johnathon cupped his hand behind Scarlett-Rain's neck and pulled her lips onto his own. Heated goosebumps surged across Scarlett-Rain's skin, like splattered drops of hot honey.

After a moment, she released her wet lips, just slightly, and began to sing to him.

"Yes, I'll be at the Calliway Fair,
where the past is but a bygone memory.
Of course, dear lad, I'll meet you there,
for you are my true love forevermore."

For where your treasure is, there your

heart will be also.

Matthew 6:21

ABOUT THE AUTHOR

Elane Peridot makes her home in the green hills of Tennessee with her loving husband and two children. She is a homeschool teacher and enjoys writing and illustrating in her spare time.

When she's not dreaming up new stories, or doodling in notebooks, Elane can often be found munching on dark chocolate, crocheting, knitting or watching old movies.

Elane's favorite subjects in school involved either ghosts or dragons, and she once lost a state spelling bee by missing the word "tibia."

Her favorite word is "wonderful," and she'd love to find a real arrowhead one day.

To contact the author or sign up for her newsletter,
please email her at:
elaneperidot@gmail.com
You can also read her blog, stay updated on new releases
and check out her other books at:
www.elaneperidot.com
♥